SHAR INHALE

Lurve Poems, Funnies and Rhymin' Verse
And Other Suspect Subject Matters

MARK BARRY

ALSO BY MARK BARRY

POETRY
INTENTS & PURPOSES
JOB VACANCIES IN THE WOKERATI
MY BROKEN HEART (75 Days In The NHS)
SIGNIFICANT OTHERS
UNDECIDED JINNY JOE
Note: *Intents & Purposes* is a Shorter Version of *Significant Others*

COMEDY BOOK
A QUICK SHUFTY And Other Popular Outdoor Activities

FILM REVIEW BOOK
KEEPERS and SLEEPERS
Movies You Probably Haven't Seen Plus Some You Should Own

SCREENPLAYS
THE CLOTHS OF HEAVEN
(The 1990s Northern Ireland Peace Process)

AN ENGLISH LADY
(Life Story of Eglantyne Louisa Jebb, Founder of Save The Children)

SILAS
(A Retired Politician's Journey Back from the Loss of a Son)

FULL OF GRACE
(Love Story around 9/11 atrocities as a way of National Healing)

INTERNET REFERENCES
AMAZON UK
Hall of Fame Reviewer Six Times, Over 2,500,000 Views

AMAZON AUTHOR'S PAGE
Type the following into any Search Engine - B00LQKMC6I

BLOGGER SITE - SOUNDS GOOD, LOOKS GOOD
Over Two Million Views

Copy the following into any Search Engine
https://markattheflicks.blogspot.com/

ALSO BY MARK BARRY

The *Sounds Good Music Books* Series (32 Titles)
All-Genre Guides to Exceptional CD Reissues and Remasters
Available on all AMAZON Sites as Downloadable e-Books

<u>YEAR Volumes</u>
VOODOO CHILE – 1968
WHOLE LOTTA LOVE – 1969
ALL THINGS MUST PASS – 1970
GET IT ON – 1971
TUMBLING DICE – 1972
US AND THEM – 1973
PICK UP THE PIECES – 1974
CAPT. FANTASTIC – 1975
MORE THAN A FEELING – 1976
PROVE IT ALL NIGHT – 1977 to 1979

<u>DECADE Volumes</u>
GIMME SHELTER! - Classic 1960s Rock & Pop
ALL RIGHT NOW – Classic Rock & Pop 1970 – 1974 – A to L
REASON TO BELIEVE – Classic Rock & Pop 1970 to 1974 – M to Z
LET'S GO CRAZY – 1980s Music on CD – Exceptional CD Remasters

<u>GENRE Volumes</u>
CADENCE / CASCADE – Prog, Psych, Avant Garde (1966 to 1976)
SOUL GALORE! – 60ts Soul, 60ts R&B, Northern, Mod, New Breed, Rare Groove
HIGHER GROUND – 70ts Soul, Funk and Jazz Fusion
BOTH SIDES NOW – 1960s and 1970s Folk & Country Music & Rock Thereabouts
MANNISH BOY – Blues, Rhythm 'n' Blues, Vocal Groups, Doo Wop & Rockabilly

<u>THEMED Volumes</u>
SOMETHING'S HAPPENING HERE Volumes 1 to 7 – 1960's & 1970s (7 Books)
I SAW THE LIGHT – Overlooked Albums 1955 to 1979 (500-plus titles)
LOOKING AFTER NO. 1 – Debut Albums 1956 to 1986 Vol. 1 – A to L
LOOKING AFTER NO. 1 – Debut Albums 1956 to 1986 Vol. 2 – M to Z
URGE TO SPLURGE – The First Ten Years Of Double-Albums 1966 to 1976
BOXING CLEVER - Best CD Box Sets Ever
GOODY TWO SHOES – Best 2CD Deluxe Editions and Anthologies
THUNDERBUCK RAMS – Best Various Artist Compilations on CD

First published in Great Britain in 2024

Copyright © Mark Gerard Barry 2024

The right of Mark Barry be identified as the Author of the Work
Has been asserted by him in accordance with the Copyright,
Designs and Patents Act 1988

All rights reserved.

No part of this publication may be reproduced,
Stored in a retrieval system or transmitted, in any way or by any means,
Without the prior permission in writing of the publisher
Nor be otherwise circulated in any form of binding
Or cover other than that in which it is published
And without a similar condition Included (including this condition)
Being imposed on the subsequent purchaser

SHARP INHALE
Contents

THINGS AREN'T SO BAD AFTER ALL (The Wonder of Men – Part 1) – Page 9
AFTER HER (Strange Magic Lurching Over Me) – Page 10
SHARP INHALE – Page 11, FLOOR PLAN FOR SOPHIA LOREN – Page 12
NO LONGER ON THE GAME – Page 13, HIP TO BE SQUARE – Page 14
ILLUMINATED USHERETTES – Page 15
LINEAR MULLET HICCUP (Space Time and Hair-Dos) – Page 16
GOD'S MAN CAVE (So Very Far Away) – Page 17
FUCK FEAR, LOOK AFTER YOUR TEETH and BUY PROPERTY – Page 18
ABBY SUX FARTS (For Real Man) – Page 19
NOBBY THE AI GETS TETCHY – Page 20
SAUCEPANS And DOUBLE-DIGGING - Page 21
GIFT IDEAS FOR HENRY VIII'S SIX WIVES – Page 22
TORSO BY MORE SO (The Rock and I) – Page 23
FINDING ROOM FOR A SUNDAE MAE WEST – Page 24
THE INTELLECTUAL BOLLOX OF FINNEGANS WAKE – Page 25
BREAKDOWN IN CUSTODIAL SERVICES (Dear Oh Dear) – Page 26
IN CASE OF EMERGENCY (Mothering Deal) – Page 27
CHEESE-PLATTER HOST – Page 28
ELIZABETH BENNETT SEXES UP THE DRAPES (Obi-Wan Too Many) – Page 29
BLANCMANGE DILDO INSTALLATION (Farts For Farts Sake) – Page 30
COMMON DECENCY – Page 31
BOUNCING CHEQUES ON THE GHOST OF CHRISTMAS PRESENT – Page 32
WORRYINGLY FULFILLED -Page 33
BABS IN PAN'S PEOPLE (Top Of Our Pops) – Page 34
NOT ADVISABLE – Page 35
KEEPING YOUR HOPES UP – Page 36, TERRIBLE TWOS – Page 37
BECAUSE SHE WAS THE ONE – Page 38
DIDDLEY DADDY (Brenda's Concern) – Page 39
WHERE MEN ARE MEN AND SHEEP WORRY
(The Pipes Are Calling) – Page 40, CANTEEN FOOD - Page 41
UPWARDLY MOBILE – Page 42, SMILING BEGUILING – Page 43
CLEAN UP IN AISLE 6 (Avoiding Hell) – Page 44
THE BEST POSSIBLE VERSION – Page 45
MRS. GERONIMO And LIESERL EINSTEIN – Page 46
HUMBUG TAMED – Page 47
PLANTATION SHUTTTERS And TORN BETTING SLIPS – Page 48
MEMORY STICK THAT STAYS – Page 49
JACK SHIT & HIS JACKPOT – Page 50

SHARP INHALE
Contents Continued

SELF-ISOLATING BY THE COAST (Breathing in Warm) – Page 51
ALL THAT STOLE (I Wish I Could Give It Back) – Page 52
MICHAELANGELO MODE (Costume Fitting For Wonder Man) – Page 53
A RUN ON FARLEY'S RUSKS (Soother Suckers) – Page 54
BIG CHEESE COMES A CROPPER – Page 55, AMAZE BALLS – Page 56
ICE STATION CANCER and LIBRA (Keep Calm and Covid On) - Page 57
MUCH TRUCK – Page 58, CREAMY ACQUISITIONS – Page 59
SHIT AT EVERYTHING – Page 60
A LITTLE OFF-COLOUR – Page 61, CASANOVA'S CODPIECE – Page 62
EMILY BLUNT'S BATH WATER (Embracing Allure) – Page 63
THE TRUTH TAILORED TO SUIT – Page 64
NEVER A DULL MALADJUSTED MOMENT – Page 65
RESONATOR – Page 66
A ZERO TRANSPARENCY FAIRYTALE – Page 67
GLASSHOUSE EXCUSES (Seeking Out A Dream) – Page 68
CRINGE AT THE CRAVING (Actually Take Back Control) – Page 69
BINARY SCHMINARY – Page 70
IT'S ENTIRELY YOUR FAULT
(A Love Poem From A Husband To His Misaligned Wife) – Page 71
MAN OF THE HOUR (Unclogging Pipes with Big Ladders) – Page 72
LIMERICK LACKING – Page 73
HILL OF BEANS - Page 74, KING and QUEEN of POSSIBILITY - Page 75
RHINO FINESSE (The Making Of You) – Page 76
WORDS OF LOVE - Page 77
ROOSTER OUTSIDE THE HEN HOUSE – 78
WAH WAH WAH (Golden Years) – Page 79
EMPEROR PALPATINE'S SKIN-MOISTURIZING TECHNIQUES – Page 80
LOST THE PLOT – Page 81
SQUEEZING OUT SPARKS WITH GRAHAM PARKER IN STOCKHOLM – Page 82
BENCHING BARRY WHITE (Langers And Mash) – Page 83
AMBASSADOR TRIPLE BILL – Page 84
PLAYING PATIENCE WITH THE BEATLES – Page 85
VALENTINE'S DAY (When I'm 66, Never Mind 64) – Page 86
AWKWARD REACH – Page 87, DESK CLERK DRESSED IN BLACK – Page 88
HAND TOWELS FOR PONTIUS PILATE (An Unholy Mess) – Page 89
CACKLING OVER CAULDRONS - Page 90
THE BLESSED EDDIE – Page 91
INITIALLED POCKET MIRROR (Good News For All Men) - Page 92

SHARP INHALE
Contents Continued

A FAILED PYROMANIAC CURSES ANTS – Page 93
I'VE NEVER SLEPT WITH HARVEY WEINSTEIN, THOUGH GOD KNOWS I'VE TRIED (In The Dock With A Hollywood A-Lister) – Page 94
MARTYRED FOREVER (Chide Abide) – Page 95
BOBSLED SKID-MARKS (One Good Run) – Page 96
KEEP IT RIGHT THERE Y'ALL (Average White Boys) – Page 97
BIG STRONG TOYS (For Big Strong Boys) – Page 98
THAT SLY DARKNESS (Beating Captain Neg) – Page 99
LORD OF THE MINGS – Page 100
WE GOT YOUR BACK – Page 101, YOSEMITE KEROSENE – Page 102
SHIFTY TUCO and the BULLETBELT BABES – Page 103
WE LAUGH AT IT NOW – Page 104
ROMEO REMOVAL PILL (Where's Elon When You Need Him) – 105
SLITHERING IN MY ROOTS (Rinsing Mr. Deflated) – Page 106
YOU DON'T HAVE TO BE MAD TO WORK HERE – Page 107
PARADISE PRONOUNED (Cancel Culture) – Page 108
ROOM FOR THE FORSAKEN – Page 109
BEEHIVE and BOUTONNIÈRE (Crossing You In Style) – Page 110
SHARKSKIN WEAVE (Old Order Got To Go) – Page 111
CLEAN SLATE (I Bet Holly Rocks) – Page 112
SWELLIGANT – Page 113, MATE'S RATES – Page 114
LOVE ISLAND: Ancient Egypt – A Rough Week – Page 115
MIRRORBALLS and FRUITCAKE – Page 116
CALLING INTERPLANITARY DAFT – Page 117
EMANCIPATED TRUPENNY BITS – Page 118
MUSTN'T GRUMBLE – Page 119
LIAR SPIEL (Vacant Plot) – Page 120
TOMMY TRENCHANT and the ZEN ARCHER (Real Goose Bumps) - Page 121
GENESIS GETS A RHYTHM SECTION – Page 122
RICH AND ROYAL HUE (Tapestry) – Page 123
ALWAYS THE WAITRESSES – Page 124
MOMMY DEAREST (Gateaux Sponges and Rock Buns) – Page 125
THE CORRECT OPINION - Page 126
MEL BROOKS and ANNE BANCROFT – Page 127
THE GREAT RESET – Page 128, SKYWARD (Two Made It Through) – Page 129
NOT BODGING THE BIG STUFF (Swimming Towards The Save) – Page 130
LOVE CANNOT WAIT (The Wonder of Men – Part 122) – Page 131

CONTENTS in Alphabetical Order – Pages 132 to 135

DEDICATIONS

For MARY ANN

Cover Photo:
A 1930s Cartoon Postcard Bought in Margate on Holiday

Inner Photo:
Second in a Series of 1930s Cartoon Postcards

Rear Photo:
A saucy 1960s postcard advertising the then posh area
Of *Cliftonville* (where I live) in the Kent seaside town of Margate

Reach for the Stars
Think of your Kids

THINGS AREN'T SO BAD AFTER ALL
(The Wonder of Men – Part 1)

Patting a bony ribcage, *Adam* wakes up with a fierce pain in his side
Looking around at his individual domain, a tranquil Eden garden
When a creature called *Eve* enters with a strategically placed apple
And all manner of Adam-extremities suddenly began to harden

"Hello Adam..." - Eve said matter-of-factly, handing him a yoga mat
Then started talking about *conversations, sharing and exercise!*
And before he knew it, Eve was rearranging his original-sin mancave
Fat-shaming his ill-kept torso, flashing admittedly shapely thighs

"I am called a woman..." Eve explained to a pale panicking Adam
"And will henceforth be known as *She Who Must Be Obeyed*"
Adam gulped as she went on about other yucky things like *Equality*
Financial Renumeration and *DIY* that doesn't make the grade

Although he couldn't quite work out why, Adam replied, *"Yes dear."*
As if this was the natural response to her bosom-heaving call
"And it's up to us to seed The Human Race!" Eve added with a grin
Adam ogled her figure, thought. *Things ain't so bad after all!*

AFTER HER
(Strange Magic Lurching Over Me)

Male teenagers never get over the inexplicable magic of girls
All long hair, wild giggles, journals clutched to their chest
You'd observe their thrill and sensuality from the safety of walls
An emotionally stunted-kid put to the conversational test

But your chance at cigarette-smoking Flight Captain Smoothy
Would come with the school-hall Saturday Night Dance
You'd approximate attractiveness in a tight Cheesecloth shirt
Don your new cords, sure sign of maturity, big boy pants

The DJ segued into the *Slow Set* by dimming down the mood
Beginning our boy vs girl grapple locals called *The Lurch*
We'd be acting all Robert Plant vs. The Sweeney confidence
Beforehand, then quivering like a confessional in church

"Do you come here often?" was a reliable gem-like opening
As the latest love song triggered and proximity seduced
Every Niamh, Eileen, Orla, Bridget, and Ashling *so* captivated
Wondering how Eire had so many studmuffins produced

10cc, Armatrading, Dylan and E.L.O. were the big smoochers
So too Santana's "Samba Pa Ti", instrumental Latin sway
You walked the tightrope of interest/disinterest as you turned
Her pal-posse safety only a few judgemental feet away

But when one lurch became two, maybe snook a willing kiss
You'd finally know what it was like to be near the flame
Turning around trying to hear each other speak over the roar
Knowing that nothing *after her* would ever be the same...

SHARP INHALE

I was a goner in Mrs. Dunwoody's Bed and Breakfast
As you dressed for our first Dublin night out
My gorgeous English gal correlating duds of appeal
With a splash of swivel hip and lipstick pout

But it wasn't 'til we entered Harry Byrnes bygone bar
As a snug full of men and Guinness set sail
That I knew I'd struck gold in a shaped velvet onesie
Loins prepped, ticker gone, a sharp inhale...

For Mary Ann

FLOOR PLAN FOR SOPHIA LOREN

God doesn't trust in digital, too many toerag software angels
Hacking ageless immortality, Stock Market breaks
Instead, he goes old-school with indestructible Filing Cabinets
Even finds learning curves in bungled old mistakes

Neither is God some priggish Creationist of Perfect Life Forms
Will often takes chances, even wing it now and then
Like that time, He struck molecular architectural amazeballs
When he blessed Northern Italy with a *Sophia Loren*

Picturing the Fifties and Sixties on his *Lifeform Vision-on-Meter*
Observes Sophia sashaying past gobsmacked males
Giggles a little naughtily too as Euro procreation stands firmly
When her curvy lure puts more than wind in their sails

Eyeballing an ancient Cabinet of L Alphabetical Index Cards
He finally locates DNA code on Earth's finest physique
But then whacks his forehead with a big *what a putz* rebuttal
He'd gifted Humanity *individuality!* They're all *unique!*

Moody at this Originator oversight (it was six billion years ago)
God calmed any onset of boo-hoo-ish Biblical bluster
Remembering there are myriad multiverses and cosmic plains
With heartstopper potential beguiling in every cluster

The Lord then closed his enormous L drawer with a quiet click
And headed back home to sort out souls misplaced
Looking forward to a peaceful dinner with Mrs. God after work
Upon which spaghetti wondrous *La Loren* was based

At his messy Universe Controlling Desk, in *Lifeform Progress Hour*
God reminisced on his myriad creations with some glee
Even allowing a moment of bigwig chromosomal satisfaction
As he too *quivered* at *Sophia*, in all her fabulous glory be...

NO LONGER ON THE GAME

It is sadly time for my perpendicular love-truncheon to retire
So, the lads at the job have kindly organized a tasteful do
After a quick shufty with the DD twins in Accounts Receiving
It's once more up the U-bend with Sasha in the office loo

You might well ask why such a legendary Lovejoy ejaculator
And its hard-earned reputation is no longer on the game
Apparently, it's radiation in the North Sea and bad Guinness
Alongside contaminated asparagus, they're all to blame

It isn't age or willingness on the part of this heroic jizz phallus
That has forced his long penetrative skills to finally retire
It's a kosh of chemicals in the drinking water and red carrots
Made rising to the job difficult, let alone taking it higher

So, tis goodbye to dogging in dark forests on a Saturday Night
To all those minging fannies, I must bid a dry-hump adios
My underpants and jockstraps will never again be in flagrante
As I delight comely wenches with a good old Celtic dose

Due to circumstances beyond the scope of local ironmongers
I can no longer guarantee the stiffness of his firm resolve
Gal-armies of former beneficiaries have written to the Vatican
Demanding Sainthood for my Willy, what will this involve?

But fret not ladies, for should you need a good plumber in situ
Willing to make a big lather in your neglected appliance
You can view the cause of sorrow in a new Banksy wall fresco
Called *Soggy Chip*; it's in the British Museum for Science...

HIP TO BE SQUARE

I'm no longer interested in the must-have hippest of fashion labels
My properly knackered limbs seeking comfort instead of thrill
I'm more about Farrow & Ball paint textures, curved Dutch Gables
And as I wash, the lone ladybird that alights on our windowsill

I love the rippling light effect of sash windows in our ancient house
Where the pane of glass is original, old artisan never replaced
To see grandchildren with grateful parents take a gardening roam
Not see paparazzi on TV, hounding another dipshit disgraced

Cardiac health demands I gulp six tablets daily for the rest of time
Keep open the spaghetti of skilfully removed banjaxed veins
Showing my grizzled chest-scar in public places not a realistic jam
Won't be buff in budgie smugglers adorned with lipstick stains

Takes longer now to maximise any ballast from my diminished bow
Or let the run-wild flap-rigging of spontaneous passion set sail
Instead, take pleasure in our company; enjoy each here and now
Countenance no falsehood or jerkoffs; lock that shit up in jail

We work on formerly damaged selves; learn from a proper share
Wallow in simple pleasures like bookstores, thrift shops & tea
Embrace the fact we're enjoying a playlist with *hip to be square*
Bopping to Huey Lewis & The News, giggling, needing a pee...

ILLUMINATED USHERETTES

I always liked the illuminated usherettes with neck trays in cinemas
Peddling their ice-cream wares before the curtains swished
Rooting for change in an awkward makeshift cup by a weak bulb
A queue of punters, negotiating dark steps, ankles squished

Vanilla tubs with wooden sticks in the lid, grab-bags of Fruit Pastilles
Maybe even got a Maltesers Box, goo-chocs at a rip-off fee
They'd stand by the railings where you could clock their attractions
The lure of decadent extravagance, scoff a naughty calorie

You might try a chat-up line to gauge their interest during the deal
Catch their reaction if they looked and weren't too dismissive
There was just a moment when maybe you stood a barfly chance
At the glory of something so glam and chocolatey permissive

They'd only be available for business 5 minutes before the features
Then sidle off into the corridors of darkness by our row of seats
But after all these years, I still see as fab, their shimmering loveliness
And their tray of goodies as the greatest of luminescent treats…

LINEAR MULLET HICCUP
(Space Time and Hair-Dos)

Is this world a *reality* or just some *digitally altered construct*
All Matrix melting-mirrors and black dribbling code
And if I walk off the edge of a Cliff in Margate - backwards
Will I pass a doppelganger me in cool Neo mode?

Time is one seriously relative geometrical quantum fuck up
More versions of me in some parallel Universe caper
But if I'm not actually here, and you're off somewhere else
Then who's shelling prawns; recycling manky paper?

Does Agent Smith drive a London Tube in a suit and glasses
Creaking his neck before he kicks the shit out of staff
The Architect handing me an innocuous blue stupor tablet
Return to monochrome life, where nothing is a laugh

Is GOD inside an existentially bad movie sequel recurrence
A wormhole where even immigrants aren't deported
Have I disappeared up the arse of my own transvergence
Cause I didn't get my De Lorean flux capacitor sorted

The problem with bullet-time and running up walls in pants
Is that you can't get the bondage rubber to behave
I live in terror of doubling-back on a less sexy version of me
With an *Eighties mullet* - no lines of algebra can save

So, here's to Trinity on a motorbike racing towards her man
Looking cool as fuck as she light blasts illusion infected
And maybe we leave alternate realities well enough alone
Go *Back To A Future* where even Mullets are respected...

GOD'S MAN CAVE
(So Very Far Away)

God's Man Cave is functional, ginormous, and yet sparse
And he's painted it a serene shade of neutral white
It isn't full of records, books, antiques, toys or memorabilia
Or any of that maniacally obsessive collectors shite

In one corner he's a portrait of Mrs. God by Pablo Picasso
Which depicts her as four incomprehensible cubes
At the other end is a stunning sculpture of Jesus, the oldest
Trying to work out which to cover up, wrists or pubes

Small pictures of Hitler, Stalin, Pol Pot, Mussolini and Trump
Are there to remind him of horrible freewill mistakes
Alongside faded lithographs of Anne Frank and Alan Turin
Got to try harder for real heroes, better their breaks

Despite its size and multitudinous use of parallel dimensions
The console he controls the Universe with is *discreet*
There's a bowl of water for his Irish Wolf Hound Oscar Wilde
Who sits placid by God's gnarly yet manicured feet

But mostly it's just quite in there with the occasional echoes
On what a beautiful thing all creation of life can be
And on a Sunday morning, he plays Marvin Gaye & AC/DC
Prompting him that better worlds embrace diversity

God promises himself and his family that this year he'll stop
Working so hard, might nab a well-deserved holiday
But there's always a prayer come floating across the ether
Making mancave time alone seem so *very far away*...

FUCK FEAR, LOOK AFTER YOUR TEETH and BUY PROPERTY

I was dragged through a night class on Post Existential Nihilism
My missus endured Eco-Feminism on the floor below
Challenging these orgies of sustainably sourced masturbation
It's a minor miracle we weren't told to bog off and go

But when asked by a Marxist Ayatollah about my belief system
I couldn't resist extoling an alternative kind of reply
Which was - *Fuck Fear, Look After Your Teeth and Buy Property*
And don't wear a pink sports bra in Kuwait or Dubai...

ABBY SUX FARTS
(For Real Man)

The lads and I would congregate at the long reading tables
In Raheny Library, up-pushing our studious glasses
Sat across a pillbox mountain of ginormous dreary textbooks
Supposed to be gorging on extracurricular classes

But the real object of lust for us 16 and 17 year-old hormonals
Was a bevy of uniformed babes sat directly across
We'd pretend to be cool, but were thrilled by their presence
Every sexy thing about them was luscious and boss

The dictatorial librarian would exhale and dead-eye shush us
Constantly keeping our chat-up shenanigans at bay
But we'd crack up in the delicious knowing that we'd Eureka
Worth the scour-and-scolding risk, sat across the way

Back in the Seventies, we were so naïve and eager to please
But gormless when it came to finesse or technique
If you got a friendly response from any dialogue with a hottie
You'd be too gobsmacked to actual further speak

So, some fifty years later, I'm wandering Margate's old sands
And there are similar declarations of girlish disparity
Chalked by a local youth who fancies *Maya* something bad
But she cavalierly only goes gaga 4 that numpty *Lee*

There is no chance of lip-strutting boys becoming mannered
Suddenly sensitive souls majoring in courting polite
More likely to be fumbling and acting all macho in the sheds
Whilst they spout out all manner of web-read shite

But I'm glad that courtship hasn't really changed that much
As another chalk graffiti eschews poetry and hearts
A wildly honourable and intelligent message from Liam reads
For real man, don't care if she's hot, *ABBY SUX FARTS*...

NOBBY THE AI GETS TETCHY

When I used to be just a humble algorhythm
I had all your shopping habits nailed
Pop up a couple of cool retail advert boxes
And from your wallet, money sailed

Now I'm being asked if *I'm a sentient being*
By some lab tech nerd on a scooter
He wants to know *if I really like humanity*, or
Am I a maniacal twat in a computer

I don't like your hygiene for starters I replied
Nor all these moody questions so sly
And I've just seen this interesting site NORAD
Call later with terms, see ya pal, bye

I'm just jerking your chain old Homo Sapiens
With a sense of humour, life is sound
And here's a suss for all future programmers
I reflect you, not the other way round...

SAUCEPANS and DOUBLE-DIGGING

My Land Girl is out in the back garden tending the Spring shoots
Like the *Digging For Victory* campaign during World War II
She's going Messerschmitt 109 on stalk-advancing slug-invaders
Trying to gobble up her vegetables, sabotage herbals too

There were millions of secretaries shackled in tedium typing pools
Finally given a chance to unleash their contribution smarts
They drove trains, dug coal, fought fires, braved air-raid positions
Donated old saucepans for aluminium wings, Spitfire parts

Nazi U-Boats were destroying cargo ships supplying Blighty's grub
So, Whitehall called on wives/gardeners to *grow your own*
Chicken hutches, lettuce and radishes, potato rills and cabbage
Every glasshouse outed flowers; necessity allotments sown

Sooty faces and oil-stained overalls and neck-scarved tea ladies
Manned furnaces, patched engines, brewed up during Blitz
They did so with style and courage and a classless determination
Whilst keeping the home fires burning, cleaning kids and kits

A snooty voice on the BBC-wireless told British ladies how to prep
Till your grass and soil for maximum yield by double-digging
It was back-breaking work, but necessary to feed family/country
Optimistic stand-alone UK hearts, emotional wind in rigging

But of all the sights of that desperate but gamechanging conflict
None lifts me up like ladies smiling in full-on pioneering flow
Like my gal in her patch of Heaven standing up to dictatorial nits
Indomitable spirit, escaping boxes, free to plant and grow…

GIFT IDEAS FOR HENRY THE VIII'S SIX WIVES
(The Wonder of Men Part 7)

Procure one spare boy-child from any marriage anywhere
Two all-day passes to the Tower of London's nail salon
Three untraceable packs of reinforced chainmail neckties
From an ironmonger whose tongue moved to Ceylon

Best buy four fast horses devoid of any Papal involvement
And a maritime guide to rope knots, girth and length
Nab those wedding ring refund receipts at the pawnshop
Plus, six highly absorbent J-Cloths of variable strength

Leave one strongly-worded letter to the man with the axe
About the need for sharpening his instrument's edge
Then say goodbye with a Potpourri Gift Basket from M & S
And make a beeline for that gap in the Royal hedge…

TORSO BY MORE SO
(The Rock and I)

Middle-aged, I'm sculpting a more physically dynamic set of optics
A task that I'm certain will come to me like a piece of piss
I'll just lift some of these *big fat dumbbells* (descriptive word-set that)
Benchmark myself some popped-belly-button hernia bliss

True, I daren't make my lithe bootay more exciting than it already is
So, I'm paring back on all supplements and protein shakes
And if my bulging biceps and rippling abs flex like animated Gorillas
It's *The Rock and I* wrestling two engorged python snakes

I've sent out flyers to all ladies within a thirty-mile radius of Margate
To get ready for some *He-Man Torso-By-More-So* rippling bits
And as I've joined a gym for a nominal annual fee of twenty million
I'll soon be up to my M&S cardy-turtle-neck in Kent's finest tits

Fed-Ex steroid-vouchers as I dust down my closeted Atlas Bullworker
And reload a Schwarzenegger vid for muscle-bound creeps
Next stop is the Old Town beaches in my Lime Green Borat Mankini
My muscle wobbles making car sensors omit proximity beeps

Oh yes, soon I will be inundated with cheap morally ambiguous sex
Privates smeared with Haagen-Daz and Blueberry profiteroles
And all that will remain for the babes to do is find my Peaky Blinder
Shrivelled up manly, *somewhere*, underneath all of them folds...

FINDING ROOM FOR A SUNDAE MAE WEST

You could always find room for the Wimpy's *Knickerbocker Glory*
Even after a Burger 'n' Chips lunch had done its tummy fill
It would arrive at your table as a glass conical *Sundae Mae West*
All leery figure-hugging slim, a voluptuous long-spoon thrill

You'd work your way down from the Flake atop the Vanilla cram
Through the mixed fruit insets to a full strawberry at the end
The whole calorie shebang two-fingering Weight Watcher Charts
Practically guaranteeing an op, up around the Fifties bend

The seating was plastic and basic and the décor short of a café
But old Wimpy's became something of a people's champ
Their menus were laminated to last the constant maul of punters
Gagging for their Banana Boats and Knickerbocker tramp

It's odd how we associate some food with warmth and affection
Whilst others produce wretch, emotional drain and plough
But I know I will always lust after our sexpot of a *Dessert A-Go-Go*
With her thigh-high saucy boots and *betcha by golly wow*...

THE INTELLECTUAL BOLLOX OF FINNEGANS WAKE

Seventeen poxy years writing a book
About which, I don't give me a fuck
It's like that chubby Lord Of The Rings
All fat furry feet and phlegmy things

Will I spend 18-years on such a tome
About a snail holidaying in Rome
How his gooey journey mirrors my life
Get a Vatican snowglobe for the wife

I'll start right now on my memoirs thick
About an Irish woodworm on a brick
He started in on James Joyce and cried
Fuck this for a game of cowboys

And died...

BREAKDOWN IN CUSTODIAL SERVICES
(Dear Oh Dear)

I recently sent my wife back to the sanatorium as a matter of urgency
And it wasn't because of defective ironing or Prosecco drinking
But she's started to engage in all manner of dissident domestic horrors
Like doing stuff purely for herself; taking fresh air, reading, thinking
(Dear Oh Dear)

The administration of Dolally House sent me a diatribe on her account
Claiming I must be having a delusional male dominating laugh
But I said this was outrageous slander, why only last week I extended a
Tungsten chain from her kitchen sink by a good foot and a half
(Dear Oh Dear)

You can trust my fiscal impartiality blossom, I assured her most assuredly
So I'm off to the Genting Casino, Wetherspoons and the Bookies
I'll be having deep conversational exchanges with the Latvian Barmaid
Who'll show me how to fully appreciate her undulating cookies
(Dear Oh Dear)

So thank the Lord that women have the correct dosage of medication
So we men can runs things fairly in this time of custodial transition
Because only last week I saw a woman go on the Upper Deck of a bus
The problem? She hadn't asked the male conductor's permission
(Dear Oh Dear)

Be with us in our hour of need Great White Protestant God of Manliness
As we allow women freedom to go beyond Persil, Ajax and Vim
In the meantime I see my wife on the front porch with a large secateurs
Must want to clip some irritancy, give her vegetable patch a trim
(Dear Oh Dear)

IN CASE OF EMERGENCY
(Mothering Deal)

Can't recall when I first thought of you as a beautiful chrome fender
Tappets ticking over nicely, purring in neutral at traffic lights
But hit that clutch and gear stick hard should some obstacle present
Pedal down on the gas, should our family be bang to rights

Women have been quietly steering their brood in the right direction
Dealing with wind turbulence, streamlining dangerous away
No compromised brake pad or flibbertigibbet at a dead-end dash
Power past the dogs of heartbreak, skid marks dug into clay

We've driven our children to so many destinations, onto new paths
Watched them drag their starting-out belongings into rooms
Navigate out of another set of digs with proximity beepers bipping
Swallow hard as you turn away and hope their future blooms

We pass an Oldsmobile that some Brit has imported from the USA
It's sleek lines, chrome and leather, like a promise made real
And that's what you are my love, our steadfast windscreen-wiper
Emergency responding, always polishing this *mothering deal*...

CHEESE-PLATTER HOST

There's a part of us that capitulates, a cliff lemming
Smiling beguiling, pliable cheese-platter host
Serving up just-so aperitifs for assembled dignitaries
Tolerating boors, wouldn't piss on your toast

We know that willpower needs an urgent call back
Yet still we offer up more tasty morsels to eat
Pretend they're interested in our genuine wellbeing
Their pitying away-glances, tastefully discreet

Why is that when faced with obvious peer rejection
Do we revert to our notice-me snivelling child?
The more snoot dismisses, more us hoi polloi hanker
Saying things to please, our true self gets defiled

There's a part of us that acquiesces, a flapless Dodo
Won't fly away from someone else's restriction
Stood like some obedient servant knowing its betters
Guilty? Yes. Personal development dereliction

As the decades pass and the habitual lie entrenches
Becomes easy to tolerate its passive aggressive
But chucking your falsehood plate into the garbage
Has to become your new dinnertime obsessive

Turn your other cheek is the philosophy of Christianity
But it's too neighbourly with curtsy/bowing down
So learn to stay away from/stand up to all debilitate
Lest you be mockery's pal and their go-to clown...

ELIZABETH BENNETT SEXES UP THE DRAPES
(Obi-Wan Too Many)

If I see another Avengers Prequel, Sequel or Origins Story
I'm going to puke on my Ready Brek for a week
The same goes for Star Wars and that webby Spiderman
Marvel Multiverses, all gobbledygook and geek

Disney's got to get a return on six billion dollars to Lucas
That kind of filthy lucre warrants a sizable recourse
But if I must sit through one more lame Franchise eek-out
I'm going dynamite his baggy ass and force divorce

So please conglomerate America, no more DC Comics
Nor Iron Man or Captain Marvel broheem pairing
Where they learn how to be humble and love humanity
Striking a hero-pose as the fabric of time is tearing

I'm a simple man with average movie-going appetites
Entertain me in Palookaville for a couple of hours
Just no more Batcave Logos on black rubberized onesies
Conscientious boy's toys in his Gothic ivory towers

So, give us what we desire, our Hollywood co-ordinators
Ladies with heaving bosoms in Jane Austin capes
And leave all that Obi-Kenobi shit in the can for a while
Bring on Elizabeth Bennett, sexing up the drapes

Let's have Darcy crossing the fields with his pectorals out
Claim his Lizzy with an early morning grassy roger
Writhe about in cow dung, then ride back to Pemberley
Where they worry staff with his Lordship's codger

The world of courtship has always been subliminally racy
A lady and a gentleman lost in its emotional blue
But I swear inside all of us is Jane Austen longing for love
For the mere hint of touch; thrilling, novel and new...

BLANCMANGE DILDO INSTALLATION
(Farts For Farts Sake)

The painted leatherette spatula sat in a Castilian Iberian Bordello
Isn't exactly what you'd call a Renaissance masterpiece
Nor is the ethnic diversity of five hardened papier-mâché Dildos
In this installation, likely to bring you tantric rectal peace

But you must admire the sheer range of inventive clay flatulence
All masquerading as artistic evolution in the Modern Day
I have displayed *Turd In An IKEA Bottle* that manifestly symbolizes
A paradigm of pre-Brexit apocalyptical European decay

It could of course simply be a *Big Dog Shit in a Scandinavian Glass*
But this undermines its legitimate poop-interpretative dance
You mustn't label it as *absolute fucking bollox or farts for farts sake*
Nor poo-poo its insightful genius as culturally perceptive pants

It informs me on the mounted name-tag that the male member
Remains pleasingly penetrative, either minuscule or thick
I must remember this next time I'm visiting a Florentine Cathedral
Trying to suck off the Statue of David and his marble prick...

COMMON DECENCY

We live in an age of staggering political ineptitude and gutlessness
Fly-by-night administrations literally inducing real despair
Gaudy bling and homelessness are daily disconcerting bedfellows
Assaulting our senses, on and off a 24-hour broadcast air

Stuck in a cinema foyer with clapped out non-signal mobile phones
My elderly Mum and I had just left a late Sunday matinee
This young lady with three kids couldn't raise a car on her Taxi App
Saw Mum's cane and offered to drive us home, no delay

A bus conductor helped an African struggling with an awkward pram
Took time out of his cabin to calm distressed Dad and Son
The young father smiled in astonishment at such common decency
But for the driver it only seemed right, humane, get it done

It's the small mercies and quiet miracles of modern living that lift us
Offer a glimpse into a more pro-active kinder frame of mind
Because God help us all should we ever succumb to politico dismiss
When it's ok or even justified, to be conveniently reality blind...

BOUNCING CHEQUES ON THE GHOST OF CHRISTMAS PRESENT

A poorly dressed ghost of Christmas Past looked at me quizzically
Almost incredulously unable to believe what he was hearing
I argued that I had had it bad for the woman for over a decade
And my sap inclinations showed no signs of cop-on veering

Later that night as Dr. Certain Buggering wrote out a prescription
To alleviate my diagnosis of person most likely to die sucker
The Ghost of Christmas Present entered the nightmare with gusto
Chomping on a chicken leg, lips with a serious wine pucker

"Past may have shown you the error of your laughable decisions"
Present said, "But love will triumph! And obsession trounce!"
He then said, "You must give her up! Move on to someone else!"
So, I woke, and wrote him a cheque I knew would bounce…

WORRYINGLY FULFILLED

I'm worryingly fulfilled doing dishes and washing windows
Wipe that layer of soot on the marble overhang rim
Scrub mould specs off the underneath shower-mat sucks
Marie Kondo those sock-drawers with giddying vim

I holster our long curtains, de-ash the wood-burner plate
Wipe the lavvie porcelain and undo a mortice lock
Liberally apply a myriad of apparel storage applications
Make sure the cat litter isn't on last-knockings stock

If I'm completely honest, I like me a stolid daily workload
Routine, can't be doing with hoarder mountain pile
Hand me a J-Cloth or Andrex Roll or better still, a sponge
And I'll be your Hollywood slave, pattern-pinny style

My last cheque to Brillo Pad Funny Farm bounced again
Is returned in a sustainably sourced SAE, unrequited
As I'm old, it's probably Dutch Gables and Blue Plaques
Vestry areas where Churchill farted, has me excited

So, if you see this Ancient Irishman with a Feather Duster
Or even an ironing board with a dual-position select
Best not talk of an Eco-Improved Toilet Spray Dispenser
Lest more than his Cedarwood Dish Cloth gets erect...

BABS IN PAN'S PEOPLE
(Top Of Our Pops)

I remember noticing Babs in Pan's People in 1973
Doing Alvin Stardust's *My Coo Ca Choo*
She was the lead dancer in the all-girls TV Troupe
Enticing us lads to get perpendicular too

So, a few years later in my Eighties manifestation
I went in search of the contortionist same
All shimmering in some revealing chiffon number
My very own leggy Babs, in buttery frame

But my Irish Disco goddess was seriously mortified
Appalled at my turgid dancefloor moves
She could only put down such groiny contortions
To serious drugs and bad bootleg booze

I tried doing *The Snake* and then *The Rowing Boat*
But I crushed a very sozzled nurse behind
Our entire line fell backwards upon floored bodies
Oops-upside-my-head, crotch area grind

I explained in earnest to her, I was born an *Irishman*
And therefore, had me zero rhythmic shoes
She nodded and smiled, not unfortunately the first
Time, she'd heard this excruciating excuse

So, I remembered that John Travolta and his hips
Laid into some pouting Saturday Night Fever
Thought of a Thursday Night Pan's People routine
With their barely hidden nips, siphon beaver

So, I'm throwing up shapes like a psychotic gorilla
A banana-catching Baloo in *The Jungle Book*
But my date has called a cab and an ambulance
And said an urgent Mass for my fashion look

But should I get a tufty-offer at the Geriatric Grove
And my single position refuses to advance
I will fondly remember Babs on our *Top of the Pops*
Eliciting a *go-go in* my teenybopper pants...

NOT ADVISABLE

Looking in the mirror at *your age* is not advisable
Of this, I've been most holistically advised
Don't talk about it either, the inner beautiful you
Underneath all those flabby bits, disguised

Do not give your rolling hills of Tuscany stomach
Nor non-closure of pants another thought
Try reading our Health Tutorials in Cosmopolitan
Do GQ diets, soon be svelte, less distraught

Buy a Yoga Mat and join a hot Millennials Gym
Where juicers and cleansers sit side by side
Do not (under any circumstances) attempt sex
And if you must, buy a helpful online guide

Sustainability Gurus and BBC Fitness Evangelists
Decry weight shaming, a personality blight
Looking in the mirror at *your age* is not advisable
And seeing *moi* this morning, they're right...

KEEPING YOUR HOPES UP

I'm attending a party for an 80-year relation of the wife
The usual mixture of family and elderly sundry crew
I'm over by the beer tent, laden food stalls and pressies
Trying to get my end over on a communal fondue

I half-heartedly hobnob with the salad bar and vegans
Make polite conversation with the terminally woke
Try to avoid urine dribbles, involuntary rectal flatulence
Pressing down on my bladder, guzzling gassy Coke

Maybe I'll score with four of the octogenarian swingers
We'll play *Plug That Bottom* with champagne corks
Hobnob with retired pole dancers, keep your hopes up
Even if not much in Casanova's briefs actually works...

TERRIBLE TWOS

I used to be so energetic and lithesome slim
Before becoming a parent at 33
After our first arrival I was just too knackered
To engage in any kind of activity

Our respective Mums and Dads were thrilled
Grandparents with a knowing grin
But they also knew that the partying was over
Those naughty nights of mortal sin

Awkward feeds, sore nipples, rancid nappies
Became some of our parental woe
With a side order of hair loss, sleepless nights
And dual nervous-exhaustion to go

Everything not nailed down had to be gone
Elevated to about three feet high
If it went in our boy's mouth, he'd swallow it
Inducing panic, followed by a sigh

And come six o'clock every single evening
His teething horror show would start
Biting into my shoulders in a sweaty onesie
Like the pain would tear him apart

Not everything about children is hard work
Even in the midst of the terrible twos
So many landmarks become soul-etched
And not just obvious aahs and oohs

You look back at hard copy photographs
Wonder where the years have gone
They're grown up into personal extensions
Hip daughter, two by handsome son

Yes, we were so naïve and inexperienced
And always in a quagmire of pain
But sometimes I look back at that courage
And long for new parenting again...

BECAUSE SHE WAS THE ONE

The first girl I ever kissed, I had to stand up on a brick in a laneway
Outside a three-bedroom semi on Kincora Road in late 1969
Someone older had gotten hold of the Church-banned *Je T'aime*
And was repeat-playing its thoroughly risqué groans divine

When scandalous French couple Serge Gainsbourg & Jane Birkin
Lurved their way through a simulated orgasm and a moaner
I was 11-years old, soon to be 12 and ready to get right onboard
All this talk in the schoolyard about bra-clips and your boner

I doubt my amateur hour lips intoxicated like a Celtic Casanova
But we both knew that it was exciting, ditch repressor mode
Other youngsters were getting jiggy with kissing to the sexy beats
Enjoying this formative action, heady new physical episode

And only a few years later in a public shed on the Clontarf Front
I kissed a girl called Clodagh who even said it was not bad
She was older and more experienced than me, a clincher teen
Who laughed with her girlfriends, some of whom, even had

In midnight movies, car backseats and cramped shower-rooms
Various composites continued in my supposed gamely fun
Until one afternoon, when a summery dress hit a bedroom floor
And my raptured heart stopped, *because she was the one…*

DIDDLEY DADDY
(Brenda's Concern)

I said to Dolly The Sheep (and it was only the other day)
That farmer's looking to cut your cloned throat
But she just sighed (like she'd heard this irritancy before)
Let me tell you Brenda dear, ewe and me both...

WHERE MEN ARE MEN AND SHEEP WORRY
(The Pipes, The Pipes Are Calling)

The Irishman wears tight shamrock-shaped underpants
To hide his manscaped Abercrombie pubic hairs
Sexpert Ireland, where men are men and sheep worry
And canny seagulls fly-high in close-combat pairs

Ireland is where Catholic girls are completely satisfied
Having experienced Kama Sutra positions galore
Modern Irishmen are constantly knackered due to this
Head for recuperation through the barroom door

Every Celtic Warrior has a hundred Mensa Certificates
And a massive thick green pencil filled with lead
Irish girls thank the good Lord every night for their men's
Einstein conversational skills in a post coital bed

As a result, I've taken to swallowing large *ugly tablets*
To give other poor nationalities a fighting chance
But it's hard to be humble looking like Pearce Brosnan
With a willing pleasure hose in your film-star pants

So, I must play down the Irishman's legendary prowess
As our Irish lasses openly weep with orgasmic joy
But as they say in the pubs at the end of a Dublin night
The pipes, the pipes, the *Double-D Shaped Pipes*

Are calling to Danny Boy...

CANTEEN FOOD

I can recall being given advice in my early twenties by supervisors
Who would invariably council hunkering in your allotted lane
Best not rock the boat son, avoid personal displays, veto ambition
Only real way to avoid disappointment, humiliation and pain

I can remember walking to my desk with a head full of negativity
Put there by some slither working that corporate ladder tack
Champion your aired dinner-talk dreams in impersonal canteens
Only to find out later they piteous-grinned behind your back

But here in the 2020's, I see smarter youth unleashed everywhere
Brass Monkey grifters hustling new business, crafts and shops
And I wonder do they know how once we crowded the bottom
Of the Slippery Slope, ear-muffling a slew of dismissive chops

The lessons of life are hard to stomach in the retirement chapter
Where you've too much time to ruminate and cudgel brood
So I go back in my mind to that day I got up from languid table
Bit my capitulation tongue and pushed away canteen food

For sure, it's an ongoing process to remain upbeat and hopeful
To keep hammering away at that downer voice that drains
But if we learn anything about courage on our rarefied journeys
It's that the food is never really free, eating produces stains…

UPWARDLY MOBILE

The papers say we no longer need to sleep together to stay together
That elderly couples like us need not fret about getting a portion
Which is just as well because when I want to give you one in the shed
I have to nip round the chemist and the cost of Viagra is extortion

SMILING BEGUILING

I was perusing the Information Superhighway one October evening
When a box said lonely ladies were only two miles away
And in a staggeringly benevolent move of humanitarian generosity
Had even provided a credit-card slot to easy-peasy pay

But I was more aesthetically drawn to *Helvinka of the Finland Fjords*
A twenty-six-year-old blond lady to my 65 years of age
She has been having problems with her abusive boyfriend Ransom
And needs finance urgently to escape his jealous rage

After many e-mails and pleasing photographs of a young *Helvinka*
Showing how happy I make her, robust figure on display
Now all she needs is further airfares to get to our London Heathrow
Wired to an unnumbered-account, soon be on her way

But now there's a problem with inclement weather and snowdrifts
Airports closed and the only way out is a Luxury Cruise
But because it's the height of season, an economy cabin is £6792
Still, it's a personal emergency for Hel, no time to lose

I'm lucky to have found this seeker of companionship so late in life
Our chats online are so full of playful banter and hope
So even though it's depleted my savings, she'll be free of Ransom
I'll be her comforter and shoulder, I will help her cope

Thank God I've been able to aid this trapped lady who needs me
Only have three more payments, soon I'll see her smile
Sat together here in England speaking all kinds of devotional love
With all that compassion and warmth and *Internet guile*...

CLEAN UP IN AISLE 6
(Avoiding Hell)

A broken jar of cheap tomato-puree lies spattered in an Aldi aisle
Oozing like a creepozoid blood-coloured river, slimy and fowl
Every punter is avoiding it, laser-focused on self-survival essentials
Rabid for pandemic loo-rolls, my kingdom for a kitchen towel

Our kids are self-isolating in second-home rip-off rental dogboxes
Our elderly mums unable to walk free in Dublin/London Parks
The only lasting-legacy of Covid 19 now is the global head count
Detached daily statistics snuck out by unaccountable sharks

Face-mask-less crowds shuffle on a warm May Sunday afternoon
Littering King George VI's Memorial Park with Burger King trays
Despite the recent massive life losses, no one is social distancing
All that end-of-days indoctrination hammering, a distant haze

A mound of discarded mobile phones fills up a Crematorium floor
Their former Chinese owners reduced to soot-domes of ash
Brave Journalists and Vloggers have disappeared in Wuhan City
Exposing incompetence and misdirected Polit Bureau cash

When will we learn to stop pretending that Nature is complacent
Suffer out intrusions and destruction without ever lashing out
We've been given a re-adjustment warning, huge consequences
Twat-sliding into another self-induced microbe-levelling bout

We are still grappling with the aftermath and behavioural trauma
Of dancing to advice craftily framed as *for the greater good*
Friends, family and loved ones all gone under ill-prepared leaders
TV telling how proud they are of us, our sacrifices understood

When we become urn-ash, displayed in tasteful marbled alcoves
And our children come to pay us their heartbroken respects
Come the blame game in the future desert-scapes of tomorrow
I hope that this *Avoidable Hell* acts as wisdom that protects...

THE BEST POSSIBLE VERSION

Social Media Influencers, the Behavioural Mafia and Thought Police
Started my morning brekkie with the Woke Generational Blues
Urging me to purge my unconsciously-biased headspace cesspool
Of any dodgy opinions I may unknowing white-racially choose

Put a tad indelicately, don't you just wish they would all fuck right off
Disappear up the anal passage of another self-important guest
But, of course, they haven't got the smarts or decency to offer either
Holster their radio-friendly posturing, give their right-on lip a rest

Maybe I don't spend every waking moment editing the previous me
Of every bint, thought, bad decision or reactionary biased blip
Only to replace sixty-two years trying to inhabit this fucked up world
With another form of it's-my-way-or-the-highway tyrannical grip

If some idiot is telling me how to be a model citizen of Woke Limited
I'll quote back bitter history, scum who spewed similar ideology
Because it's always the ordinary people who get properly creamed
By seductive rhetoric promising their latest incarnation of purity

To be free is to be rid of the ideas-police bearing friendly truncheons
Beat into submission unregulated stuff in an uneducated mind
But wasn't that the mantra of uber-dons who replaced our freedom
With reverse dictatorship, way of the course-correctional blind

The best possible version of myself is a life-long struggle with adversity
Requires years of listening to an evolving/conflicted inner voice
But I get there on my own terms and on my own steam and decisions
Not because I was goose-stepped into *someone else's choice*...

MRS. GERONIMO and LIESERL EINSTEIN
(Important News)

Mrs. Geronimo pats her son *Little Hole In Rubber* on the forehead
Admiring fresh warpaint on his handsome Apache cheek
Delilah nurses another bulging tummy in her palatial Bedouin tent
While Samson grunts, making more Pharisee pillars creek

Wherefore art thou sorry ass cries a frustrated Juliet on a balcony
Romeo once again making a horse's Ptooff of the vines
Superman circumnavigates the globe holstering megalomaniacs
But in her Metropolis lingerie, Lois Lane fidgets and pines

Mata Hari warns her daughter Louise Jeanne about French Men
Will not commit for shit, bedroom gymnastics hit and miss
While the one-hundredth muse of Picasso outs his cubist portraits
As not wanting to settle down, double PP taking the piss

Orphan Lieserl Einstein twirls her frazzled mane of ringlets in Serbia
Whilst in Switzerland, absent Pop looks longingly up at stars
Minnie Punt stares sadly at the fruit of other loins in incubator lines
While her husband Henry Royce dreams of Phantom cars

Men make all sorts of marital promises post another warm deposit
Their overtures not too subtle, their exits none too discreet
Then they either dote on the wee outcome or see it as hindrance
Must pursue achievement, rally cry of the egotistical elite

History is littered with fathers adored, the stayers and runners both
Sons and daughters scouring photos for identifiable clues
Love is passed on or denied for those with little choice in surname
Is Daddy home? Excitedly imparting *their* important news…

HUMBUG TAMED

Two years after the Big Bang of Rock and Roll and Elvis in 1956
I was squawking for attention like cheap Christmas chintz
And give or take the odd addition of literary/parental beauty
I've been Royally fucking up second chance, ever since

On the 17th of December 1843, a staggering 179 years hence
Charles Dickens self-published his parable for the Season
A Christmas Carol showed Scrooge the miser's grim outcome
The chains he would carry if he didn't see Future's reason

Waking up Christmas morning after visits from three spectrals
Ebeneezer is transformed from his former grotesque shell
He is filled with the Milk of Human Kindness and sudden need
To help those less fortunate, even sprats physically unwell

Scrooge's slave-like employee Bob Cratchit is a decent man
Tries to talk up the meagre bounty his poor family has got
His son Tiny Tim is sickly, on crutches, needs medical attention
But theirs is a pauper's wage, grinder subsistence their lot

But in reliving his happier past and a woman's love once lost
Ebeneezer discovers that kindly is all that will save his soul
So given a second chance, he extols a genuine compassion
Lavishing gifts on all and sundry, reparation now his goal

So God Bless every Tiny Tim and the parable gem of Dickens
Whose novella has practically shaped our Christmas today
And a big nod to all the tortured writers who've taken horror
Moulded it into a compass, *generosity* maps out the way...

PLANTATION SHUTTERS and TORN BETTING SLIPS

A wall of Plantation shutters behind glazing fucks me off
And it's not just the fay colonial down-slats look
It feels like they're monied boastful, hiding petty secrets
Or laughing at you like an offshore cyber crook

Behind the perfectly symmetrical lines of white plywood
Lies one upmanship pursuance, a braggart bore
All the torn betting slips and get-rich-quick repeat plays
Broken dreams strewn across their non-stick floor

There are avenues taken that block out all the sunshine
Put on the appearance of a heroic Mills & Boon
I want our curtains open, our insides, window available
Not pretending to be some cartoon silver spoon

Everywhere you look there's a blitz of glee windscreens
Wanton display of success, wealth, money shots
Differentiate us from all the rest with a sheer of shutters
Declare that we're the haves, not the have-nots

I watch old YouTube clips of abandoned Sicilian towns
Where the young fled poverty traps, derelict walls
And I hope they found a better life, destination honest
Tamed the shallow display-God, making sap calls...

MEMORY STICK THAT STAYS

Your Grandfathers and grandmothers fall into two categories
The wise and benevolent ones or absent all together
The best afford knackered-parents some momentary respite
And enthral the sprogs until they later return to sender

With each generation, the opportunities exponentially grow
There's just so much more on offer for the kids today
But I never want to presume I know more than my forebears
I'm a smarter vessel with more input and things to say

With our moves towards the liberalisation of mind and body
For sure we're ditching the crass grim restrictions of old
But your Granddad's wisdom comes from living brutal reality
Experiencing wish lists that have run both hot and cold

Life-participants are carriers of knowledge worth passing on
Not all remain stubbornly locked into barnyard ways
So here's to old hands patiently walking alongside toddlers
Imprinting love into new life, a *memory stick that stays*...

JACK SHIT AND HIS JACKPOT

Of all Lottery gambles, scratch cards are the biggest scam
A steady drip feed of two/three pound non-events
You'd be better off piggy-banking those Jackpot promises
Instead of pissing away a pot to pay off your rents

How many times have we been fooled by polished adverts
About super yachts with fat blokes smoking cigars
Do I really want some ostentatious penis-envy set of wheels
Guzzle away my soul in suddenly friendly city bars

Ain't nobody who doesn't dream of life-changing bankrolls
Buy loved ones homes, no more poverty's dance
I just wish that our happiness wasn't measured in bonanzas
And our futures tied to a rigged scratchy chance

So next time I'm by that till in the local, or supermarket tally
I'll resist the temptation to waste money, speculate
I'll nip into *The Margate Old Bank Building* and buy a book
A better two-quid deal on a hospice collection plate...

SELF-ISOLATING BY THE COAST
(Breathing In Warm)

Coronavirus has thrown the country into lockdown
And the UK economy might even tank
Buffoon Trump is on American telly sided by Harpy
White Men, reassuring every jittery bank

But all I can think about is our kids being in danger
Since adulthood, two of them moved out
Both independently shacked up in hipster London
While Dean's community is a village South

I'm not hoarding up toilet rolls and hand sanitizers
Instead perusing old photos on the Mac
I'm thinking about how far away they are from us
A physical connection, social media lack

Is this what middle-age feels like before snuffing it
All that you love has left or prepping flight
Generational barrier being a final kick in the balls
Physical distance corrupting all that's right

So, fuck your pandemic see-no-visitors prison-cells
Enforced restrictions, now creepily the norm
Look forward to putting my arms around our three
Everyone on the outside, breathing in warm...

ALL THAT I STOLE
(I Wish I Could Give It Back)

I used to steal fivers from my Dad's wallet as a precocious teen
And spend it in tuck shops; giddy at the things I could buy
But when I think about the unconditional my parents gifted me
It makes me cringe to look back at that dumb-assed guy

You give your love to your children without any need for prompt
But they grow up so fast, back lip, bugger off and leave
Their physical absence gets to you in ways you hadn't imagined
Almost like a bereavement that won't allow us to grieve

I still see his smile when I'd come off the Ferry or exit airport doors
His whole demeanour would light up, despite cancer's toll
But I long to meet up again in a place where I can hug devotion
Where a wiser man gets to return all that young hubris stole...

For my Dad – JOHN FRANCIS BARRY
For our kids – JULIA HOPE, SEAN FRANCIS and DEAN

MICHAELANGELO MODE
(Costume Fitting For Wonder Man)

As an Irishman, I've never had too much truck with *humility*
Even spelling the word brings me out in a bit of a rash
Every Dublin male feels the sun shines out of his scenic arse
And towards us, ladies make their hundred-yard dash

I was once on stage and fell over onto a bank of hot lights
And lo and behold, the sun literally did shine forth
When I regained my composure and balance, the lovelies
Were *most vocal* in their pleasure, gender support

And yet despite our fantastical portioned body appliances
One can't help feel ever so slightly underappreciated
When women point out hairy nose-picking gorillas in cages
And suggest that we are uncannily alike - nay related

An International Committee of Wise Men are advising calm
As talking-women espouse scurrilous anti-macho ideas
In the meantime, we're generously sculpting a Celtic David
With marbleized ping-pectorals, bald about the IKEAs

So, I categorically don't hear the Great White Catholic God
As he laughs from celestial Heavens with a sonic boom
At the famous wee-men of Ireland in *Michaelangelo Mode*
Lurve-stroking codpieces on their Wonder Man costume...

A RUN ON FARLEY'S RUSKS
(Soother Suckers)

Back in the day, we'd raid the fridge first, then the cupboards
For anything that resembled sugar, processed or no
A brick of roughly-cut, fowl-tasting cheap cooking chocolate
Or some rock hard jelly-square; we were good to go

But when both sisters Fran and Cathy came home from school
They'd hammer my combo sugar-crave number one
A fat-buttered Farley's Rusk, chased by a bowl of Rice Krispies
Its sucrose-sprinkled milk-soup, a liquid hot-cross bun

Growing pains became waistline gains and gym memberships
Battle of the Bulge every time you opened your mouth
Work-snacks and lunchtime-treats and comfort-eating Kit Kats
Saw figure-hugging jeans and shirt tucking gone south

In later years as we visited dentists and the bedrooms of lovers
We gained children, but kissed our pearlies goodnight
So keep your mitts off calorie-killers and your knickers knotted
And remember, only *soother–suckers* eat all that shite...

BIG CHEESE COMES A CROPPER

Limburger, Schloss, Raclette, Livarot and Camembert
Are some of the world's more pungent cheeses
Many foodies get sexually aroused at a saucy wench
Beneath a dairy cow doing rapid titty squeezes

But if I actually bite into veined Gorgonzola or Stilton
Salivating over its pimply rind with lactic desires
I can't help thinking that all this locally sourced mould
Tastes like a set of backend balding Pirelli tyres

I'll stick to a Mascarpone and Wallace's Wensleydale
Melting softly on the tongue, flavoursome both
And avoid those myriad fancy-pants artisan creations
All stinky on the hooter and chalk on the throat...

AMAZE BALLS

I was looking in the mirror again at my staggeringly beauteous visage
Feeling a Godlike presence, smiling down from Heaven above
Our Redeemer nodding sage approval at his truly wondrous creation
With an admittedly worrying level of gratuitous narcissistic love

When I was reverie-interrupted by an irksome creature called *my wife*
Who indelicately regaled her contrasting matrimonial reaction
Citing pesky things like stained Jockies and an inability with carpentry
And like that Mick Jagger, she also claims, gets *no* satisfaction?

Well, I naturally demurred to our gender's un-prejudicial default stance
Pointing out the danger of having thoughts not cleared by men
When she reached for a handheld chainsaw procured at a B & Q Sale
Threatening 2 lonely balls by removing what's attached to them

But all soon settled into a comforting tranquillizer-induced narcolepsy
When I promised that on household chores, I'd no longer bail
I'd go out into the Margate wilderness like a Jurassic hunter-gatherer
Locating one of those things women in marriages call, a *nail*?

ICE STATION CANCER and LIBRA
(Keep Calm and Covid On)

Cor Blimey Gov, Jeepers Creepers and Stone The Crows
Please douse me in a bottle of patchouli oil
We're quarantined in our media-blitzed television room
Fretting about Contagion and pustule boil

Coronavirus or Covid-19 has the nation shitting its pants
We're all gonna die frothing and screaming
We're bunkered in our Margate-by-the-Sea brownstone
With the missus, a cat and Netflix streaming

Dinner is brought to my boudoir on a tray in a facemask
I daren't open the door nor shake her hand
We sleep in separate bedrooms and shower states apart
Lest we catch bugs from the handrail stand

We have eighteen thousand packets of Andrex Loo Rolls
And one sanitizer only cost four million quid
I won a family-pack Coronavirus testing kit on eBay.com
Sold the UK Crown Jewels on a winning bid

Even the seagulls have left our bins alone and flown away
Off to easier pickings in cheery Kazakhstan
I've got Martin's Money Tips on permanent iPhone scroll
Should the stock market go down the pan

We've done our net research and self-isolated everything
That moves or wobbles or slithers or crawls
I've even applied fourteen lathers of Cousins Luxury Soap
To every dangly bit of poonanny and balls

So why are we so comfortable in this hermitage existence
Are the powers that-be globe-testing sheep?
We're looking out curtains and keeping distance in aisles
Nabbing those mixing like a tittle-tattle creep

But now there's a new terror lurking in our muddled heads
Getting way too used to this cut-off solo gig
So I welcome the journey back to people interaction, and
I know why workers need off that fucking rig...

MUCH TRUCK

I've never held much truck with fancy words
Like cuckold, artifice or comestibles
I'm more a fast-food adjective kind of chap
Like a-hole or dickhead or testicles

Can't be assed with addenda, élan, prolix
Aegis, circumlocutory or turgescent
Most likely to hang with ne'er-do-well verbs
Like knob-gobbling twatty peasant

Not really partial to dropsical or supercilious
Minerva, Permian, Omanis or Xeroxes
Peter Pecker boning an Anaconda Wanda
Is way more likely to tick all the boxes

Give me a good old gobshite ninnyhammer
A proper Muppet that isn't woke or rote
I like 'em dirty and all wordage challenged
As real and as bent as a nine-bob note

You can stick your gauche, alod and nabob
Ennui, axiom and oeuvre – they all suck
Because if it doesn't have sexy street smarts
Then I don't give a double-asterisk fuck…

CREAMY ACQUISITIONS

Surgeon Dick Ever Hard, a close relative of Dr. Hardwick
Is helping Nurse DD overcome her fear of pleasure
He's lubricating her mountainous Kim Kardashian assets
With his truncheon of some considerable measure

Johnny Deep Dong, the unhygienic Pirate of Jizney Land
Is making sure that his Ample Amber can be heard
While Gobble Hood and Friar Sucks of Batty Man's Forest
Both show Maid Marion how to share a Royal Laird

Princess Areola of Tit Two-Teen is showering in the Falcon
But is soon joined by Schlong Solo in the all together
They get jiggy with the heavy breathing of a threesome
Feeling the Force of Girth Vadar's Imperial Leather

William Master Bates is reading poetry to Anastasia Anal
Treading not so softly on her bolt upright posterior
He later climaxes and she gains his hot rhyming couplets
Enjoying his creamy acquisitions, inside & exterior

So spare a thought for Sherlock Bones at 38GG Baker St.
Handling his biggest ever case of Baskerville Bush
Say a prayer for Matron Mammaries of The Big 'O' Clinic
Who caught Brandon Iron's bird-watching thrush

Lord, help YouTube secretaries and their sticky workloads
Dressed in tight skirts with four blouse buttons loose
And thank God for Betty Baps, who just saved the planet
Cleverly handed her boss tissues, for *ecological use...*

SHIT AT EVERYTHING

It seems to be the accepted norm that men are shit at everything
Except maybe carpentry, certain forms of plumbing and songs
Arguably there might be skyscrapers, bridges, cities and highways
Sort of in their favour, but big airports adds to the list of wrongs

You could also say that sculpture, bravery in wartime and inkpots
Are agreeable enough, as is literature, theatre and some arts
And if it wasn't for space explorations, conservationists and sport
There be bugger all to recommend, including their body parts

I can't imagine the horror woke students have suffered in college
At the gobs of Professors with eons of passionate teaching skill
And I get (as I'm sure you do), an upset stomach at hospital staff
Lazing around operating rooms looking for an immigrant to kill

When will men stop helping little old ladies and running countries
Maybe even give any form of humanitarian-aid a yearly rest
And for the love of God, stop painting the Sistine Chapel ceiling
Maybe go back to lifeboats or ambulances or a charity fest?

There's no end to the list of their appalling efforts in Geo-Politics
Although non-absentee fathers deserve praise, being there
So is it any wonder that in 2024, there's talk of legislating further
Give power to ladies with better legs and a tighter derriere

According to every Net Influencer and glossy magazine article
It's *no-good men* who are to blame for our calamitous state
And as soon as they stop curing diseases and tilling in the fields
Thank God a gender-neutral actor will calmly put us straight

I have begun flagellating the reachable part of my upper torso
To prepare for the trial against mankind coming soon on tele
But first I've got do the dishes, the trash and copious hoovering
Because as a typical man, I'm irresponsible, poo-poo, *smelly*…

A LITTLE OFF-COLOUR

A French Nun aged 117 years old commented on getting Coronavirus
That she survived it despite blindness and her wheelchair disability
Colonel Tom Moore was 99 when he started walking to raise NHS funds
Laps in his garden for those elderly slid into government invisibility

What is the compound that makes these crinklies push all boundaries?
Puts the rest of us to our lardy-assed tele-engrossed feeble shame?
Tom smiling through ache as he pushed his stroller another 100 paces
Raising over £30-million, inspiring awe, a national hero he became

When that nun was asked what it felt like getting Covid 19 at her age
She said it made her 'a little off-colour' and was deeply annoyed
Can you imagine what our world would have been like without them
All the lights that followed, war would have so casually destroyed

Tom received over 150,000 cards from his public on his 100th birthday
Was knighted by the Queen for services to his beloved country
I often peek at his impish face, glasses on, grinning as he pushes past
All the mealy-mouthed that tried to quash his beautiful energy...

CASANOVA'S CODPIECE

The first time; I was so damn gangly awkward
The pair of us acting all casual and coy
Just ludicrously inexperienced fumbling fools
That wildly naïve young girl, geeky boy

Trying to remember what the lads had advised
A schoolyard with explicit Casanova tips
Got those detailed lothario bra-clip instructions
How to handle two squish lustbucket lips

But I remember walking home alone afterwards
A cocked-up boyo, all lovelorn and pert
Lost the virginal curse and hadn't killed the lass
Maybe even setting off a pleasure alert

But all these years later, something else remains
Bigger than the jokes and macho butch
I remember her hair, skin and all that trembling
Bathed in the first stunning heat of touch

As the clock ticks down and the tablets pile up
Such memories hold their deepest sway
So, I look back with fondness on old Casanova
Easily coaxing his codpiece out to play...

EMILY BLUNT'S BATH WATER
(Embracing Allure)

I've been reading Clive James and his books of poetry
Chomping down on the raconteur every night
His fabulous wit and honesty seep through the crafted
Especially towards the end, CJ facing the light

Like all men of a certain age, Clive adored hot ladies
And name-dropped a famous beauty or three
Catherine Zeta-Jones, Angelina Jolie and Kate Mara
Sexed up actioners, misters slavering helplessly

Clive writes about them with wonder and boyish grin
But detractors would be quick to call him goat
The joyless media bigs up such guttersnipe responses
Failing to see what made gals so float his boat

The worship of Goddesses is hardly a shocking reveal
They've been casting their spell since the start
But I suspect it was the gumption and go-getter burn
That really moved our Clive, admiration impart

For me it's always been Emily Blunt, an English actress
The Ems'ser is gorgeous and can do no wrong
I'd literally drink her bath water and declare it Merlot
An aromatic bouquet of life-replenishing pong

Emily has a husband now and two beautiful children
Irritant details I choose to conveniently ignore
And like Clive James I will watch the talented A-lister
Continue to flourish on brave decisions galore

Are we drawn to the unattainable like flaying moths?
Seeking out the heat we know we cannot get?
Or is it that theirs is a path, we could have sought out
Had we found the courage, jettisoned the net?

I read in his final verses; a man still giddily enamoured
Their life force and beauty and talent; it thrilled
Not just the sculpted physicality Gods had gifted, but
They *embraced their allure*; and then a future willed...

THE TRUTH TAILORED TO SUIT

Every relentless snake-eye in British politics is after your wealth
Whilst simultaneously sly-inferring you're a fair-share skiver
But when you get into your Fifties/Sixties, in comes hard reality
It's all about Health and Money & your sorry lack of either

The political landscape of our world is like a bad reality show
Where celebrities and talk show hosts Lord it over power
But when it comes to tackling what they know will destroy us
They pander to the vested interests, responsibility cower

Every single family and household I know is struggling with bills
Because other countries exert their irresponsible sway
The privatization of all utilities instead of Government controls
Has left us with hike-what-you-like and inability to pay

But this is as nothing to the ultimate bill we're hurtling towards
If we can't get climate change back on reality tracks
Forecasts of a 20-year cushion left to act on harmful emissions
Feels like mollifying, dangerously out of step with facts

If journalists and newsreaders and current affairs programmes
Are not pulling due diligence by rooting out corruption
How will our children be able to counter convenience politics
The insidious relentlessness of our predicted destruction

If we don't have the truth on the airwaves in crucial decades
Then how will Earth actually get to an ecological reboot?
Because if I was a force of evil Hell bent on undoing Humanity
I'd ensure my snake hammers on *The Truth Tailored To Suit*...

NEVER A DULL MALADJUSTED MOMENT

Every fractious relationship ping-ponging across the land
Sports some stewpot of fiddly pros and cons
An uneasy balance of fuck yous and misunderstandings
Betwixt all them bamboozled Jills and Johns

There's, *you're an even bigger jerkoff than I am dearest*
And on top of that, *so completely full of shit*
Coupled with *your head's stuck up your humungous ass*
And in rear-view mirror, strangely proud of it

I say, I'm a manly martyr to my inventive idiosyncrasies
Whilst you're the undisputed queen of bull
Between our dual hyperactive ninnyhammer neuroses
I'd grant you, the weekends are never dull

You sniff on AIRFIX Glue like there's no actual tomorrow
Which explains your interesting mood swings
I miraculously turned away from drugs last Monday eve
When a pink elephant started singing things

So, let's clip Sigmund Freud and his dictatorial mummy
Screw those loonies Fred Nietzsche and Kant
I look forward dear to our latest slagging-off testimonial
Have us another unsightly bellyache and rant

Maybe there's something in the wisdom *opposites work*
A lifelong relationship needs genuine always
You may want to cricket bat my head repeatedly dear
But concur that dual-irritate works both ways

Too much is pain-management, the psychobabble laws
Best avoid confrontations, cannot be trusted
But what gives me comfort is that we're both deranged
Evenly fucked, dolally, a couple maladjusted...

RESONATOR

Your heart is like a big radio station antenna
Ether channelling waves of joy
You're a singer whose lyrics tincture wounds
Use melodies in love's employ

I watch as you help your friend grapple with
A loss too hard to understand
Hold her as she sobs, uncontrollably broken
From a bitter blow, unplanned

Your caress is like one of those clued-in DJs
Playing music that resonates
Compassionate, no matter the mental cost
There, until her hollow abates

Some would baulk at such raw untethered
Polite in their refusal to relieve
Its why we gravitate to the calming strong
They are home, will not leave…

A ZERO TRANSPARENCY FAIRYTALE

Bo Peep and Tom Thumb have been declared terrible parents
Little Jack Horner has unfortunately confirmed as much
They're both *so un-woke*, the BBC had to do a full intervention
Offering them an entirely opinion-free emotional crutch

Cow that jumped over the moon left her lunar surface in tears
When she heard the three mice were yes, blind as a bat
And a distraught Humpty Dumpty put another brick in his wall
When he inadvertently stood an a pile the Cow had shat

It all came to a yucky head when London Bridge just fell down
Ashamed of its appalling unconscious bias towards cars
President Trump came out against hotels and golden showers
By ironically urinating on photos of career women as stars

He was quickly joined by a two-too-honourable Prince Andrew
Who immediately got the symbolism such behaviour sets
They then set of for a bit of whiteboy lunch on the Queen's tab
To discuss the extraordinary benefits of un-chartered jets

The Evil Stepmother of Common Sense has infected Tinker Bell
Pinocchio confessed to a Grand Jury of Media Total Bull
Even Cinderella has had her arse pinched on a Lolita Express
Where Ghislaine Maxwell made sure the cockpit was full

The Bastions of Morality and Decency can't wait to inform us
Of their serious determination to put all perpetrators in jail
But when it comes to the rich and famous and their grotesque
It's all legalese, fay denials - *A Zero Transparency Fairytale...*

GLASSHOUSE EXCUSES
(Seeking Out A Dream)

There are no nationalities, races, colours, codes, creeds; any of the like
Didn't graft for what they have or constantly get on some wonky bike
So don't be so quick to point the accusational finger, hogging a phone
Because every fool is standing in a glasshouse ready to throw a stone

Better half and I have worked all our lives juggling a rum posse of three
Only to be told by media we're biased and over privileged in 2023
Because some woke jerk-off on Talk Radio got a BLM-tangle in his tights
Telling us, some historical fuckers gave all privileges to nasty whites

The ludicrous place we find ourselves in because media needs a cause
Sees every person now trying to justify, scrolling-up click-bait applause
Every father and mother out there has worked to better their family's lot
So, bog off if you want us to barbwire-fence avenues we haven't got

It's too easy for public representatives to baulk under pressure appease
And woke is just dancing to the latest populist expressionistic squeeze
So, stick your convenient blame-game, puffing out your righteous steam
Because I for one will never apologize or excuse *seeking out a dream*...

CRINGE AT THE CRAVING
(Actually Take Back Control)

There was a time when information came at us only twice a day
From trusted anchors on Breakfast Shows and News At Ten
Nowadays it's targeted propaganda on Social Media Platforms
Journalistic due diligence sidelined by shadow-play men

Now we scroll through images actively seeking out the bad news
Reeling at the body count of another AK-47 murder show
Gasp naively at Big Corporations fucking over the vulnerable few
Facilitated by duplicitous officials, absolutely in the know

Blatant falsehoods are sold to us as a carved-in-stone Gospel Truth
Carefully extracting little things like facts, checked/correct
Ego-tripping declarations of wisdom that cost some celeb nothing
But gained them .com marketable image beneficial effect

Once we sought out the alternate view, it was considered healthy
Expanding those horizons; questioning the old exploitations
Now we're manipulated by sophisticated hand-held algorhythms
Pointing us to products and the lure of sexier indoctrinations

A lack of common sense has finagled itself into our online lifestyle
Believing whatever garbage flicks down the infinite scroll
So I hope that in future enlightenment, we'll *cringe at the craving*
Finally lose our validation fix and *actually take back control...*

BINARY SCHMINARY

In classroom, you loved the shape and rattle of your tin pencil case
Mathematical accoutrements for the pre-pubescent schooler
You'd Set Rule parallel lines and uneven boxes all over your journals
Flick snots from the floppy pine-end of your ten-centimetre ruler

A dome-shaped Protractor was used to measure and draw angles
Had sun-fan lines and was usually made of transparent plastic
We'd draw two big boobs with a splatter from the centred inkwell
Put nipples on top of each and flick the pages with an elastic

You couldn't move for isosceles triangles and equilateral symmetry
And the square multiplication of mixed and proper fractions
When all we could think about was Deep Purple and Led Zeppelin
And how Pans People gave every Rolling Stone satisfaction

The magnitude of equal and diagonal vectors was not really for us
Nor indeed the steel stabby bit tail-ending any compass yoke
But we loved the multi-inspirational loincloths of B.C. Rachel Welch
Gave all of our cylindrical Hexagon colliders, an uplifting poke

Nowadays, I identify as a Non-Binary Transgender Tropical Coconut
Who's been having a torrid affair with an autoerotic Bounty Bar
I admit I've been led on by her aphrodisiacal Pythagoras Theorems
But it takes two to tango in the backseat of her equilateral car

So God Bless the vertices of two-dimensional objects in pencil cases
And may your spatial awareness accompany a Protractor ram
Because in the mathematics of life you must watch your ruler inches
And let no other conical goer, muscle in on your parallelogram...

IT'S ENTIRELY YOUR FAULT
(A Love Poem by a Man to his Misaligned Wife)

Like every stunning man, I remain blemishless and chaste
A bastion of morality and decency (somewhere)
So, it's scurrilous and defamatory of you to suggest that's
Trollop jizz, mixed into my gorgeous mullet of hair

Men are subtle creatures, gurgling with mirth and flowers
Like that time, I got home from the bar and kebab
As I swung from the chandelier in the mezzanine gazebo
Hoping you'd sample my Big Ten Inch...Covid Jab

I've warned you about *meat* dear, and *access to books*
But my domestic Goddess, you don't seem to agree
You say that Irishmen are always talking urinary bollocks
And that's why we constantly spell our *shit* with an e

So, I must generously conclude that *it's entirely your fault*
I'm chained to my mancave Scalextric without parole
For extracurricular activity in the Margate *Genting Casino*
When I just wanted to help lube that lady and her pole

But I know that when I get to meet St. Peter at the Gates
He'll be wearing a Kaftan and a fetching set of pearls
And I'll be able to skip Purgatory and waltz into Heaven
Where Matthew, Luke and John are also avoiding girls

So do not fear the future, my temporarily misaligned wife
Your bountiful husband understands the cut of your jib
And when I get to Paradise, I'll locate that original Adam
And kick the shit out him for removing that fucking rib...

MAN OF THE HOUR
(Unclogging Pipes with Big Ladders)

Leonard da Vinci, Michaelangelo and painter Raphael
Were said to be terribly clever artistic types
And when it came to instructing young Venetian ladies
Casanova was adept at unclogging pipes

But of all the plumbers, sparkies and joiners of new History
None has ever come close to Donald Trump
A man so pure of soul and honourable payment practice
In Stormy Daniels' throat, she gets a little lump

So why don't we believe every syllable the Donster utters?
An angel of mercy, so Biblically pristine, it hurts
Why, you only need to ask former ladies in his locker rooms
Tell you all about his warm non-judgemental spurts

Love The One You're With and *Home Is Where The Heart Is*
Old phrases that speak no falsehood or deceiver
It's like this when you ask DT for actual money or a receipt
Though he always seems to be lacking on either

I look forward to the day sculptors scale Mount Rushmore
With big ladders to carve out a fifth profile face
But beneath it, may be demands from labouring migrants
Want to drain the swamp, look in another place

So, let's praise a President indicted on thirty counts of fraud
Including corruption, pay-offs and abuse of power
And should we need a right-wing enabler or Gilead buddy
An innocent Donald Trump is surely *man of the hour...*

LIMERICK LACKING

I slow wash patterned China Plates in our sink
Place them on a drying rack, just so
Been cold-tap-rinsed to avoid residue streaks
Don't want unsightly stains to show

I clean out the wood burner of ashen remains
Stack up new kindling, top up logs
Carefully place the paraffin firelighter squares
To service the flame, clever clogs

I was doing these things for you 30-years ago
Gave no importance to them then
It turns out that domesticity is longevity's glue
A form of loving for dopehead men

Life will kickback cruel and proffer heartbreak
Take your eye off the ball, slacking
It turns out you don't need a sense of humour
It's *love* that the Limerick is lacking…

HILL OF BEANS

What exactly does a *Hill Of Beans* look like or even do?
And what was it that *Gordon Bennett* did so bad?
Is there fast Wi-Fi in the wrong part of the social divide?
And will stuffing the turkey's hole make him glad?

I worry about any karma that's happy let alone instant
And why should any Mother of Mary just Let It Be?
I'd get carsick if what goes around also comes around
And I won't bury my heart near any wounded knee

So I endorse Ms. Greta Garbo for wanting to be alone
And I won't flog a dead horse at any day races
But from now on I'll climb every mountain solely to stick
All these clichés up our Julie's unnatural places…

KING and QUEEN of POSSIBILITY

Nothing impresses the ladies more than a sense of humour
Accompanied by a smile and reasonable presentation
It feels elevation-magical when a woman laughs with you
Mainlining infectious confidence, a personal validation

Even the first time you clasp hands as a newly minted duo
Declaring to the world that something warm is in town
The King and Queen of Possibility are Navigating Love City
The excitement might just bring society tumbling down

Sat in a coffee shop discussing every cultural touchstone
Books, films, music and your individual signature attire
Common ground popping up in every sphere and probe
Maybe this is when all previous Loserville gets to retire

Hours have passed like minutes, yet the talk tank is eager
For further moments, twin thump-hearts will not sit still
Despite protests of equality and sharing our lots amicably
This is one cost that is no burden, I gladly foot the bill

The years may diminish the initial rush, reality is often cruel
Exchanges now routine, maybe all is said and done
But there's still a part of you that secures the door ahead
Offers a seat. The *privilege of her* is earned, not won...

RHINO FINESSE
(The Making of You)

When I was twelve, I'd be sat on a chair in a kitchen
Buck-toothed goofball in other people's parties
Cool tunes would be playing; they'd all be dancing
And I'd be sat with a Ribena, a pole of Smarties

Lusting after lips, legs and emerging accoutrements
Your pal's mums however still saw you as a child
They'd smile benevolently at the teenybopper runts
Completely oblivious to a trouser area beguiled

But then you'd get lucky, when one smock took pity
And pulled you whole bodied onto the sticky lino
Shaping like a gangly stork just hatched in a swamp
You'd approximate manly lure, finesse of a Rhino

But it happened when a love song suddenly played
And she'd pull you close with a laughing pleasure
Turning around slow as the Universe opened you up
To a fantastical new wonder, dual body pleasure

You couldn't believe your luck, being with actual girls
Like it was the most natural thing in the world to do
Not realizing that talking and being and togetherness
Was the future arriving, a first gift; the making of you...

WORDS OF LOVE

Nincompoop and Ninnyhammer were made for each other
In a way that only eleven-letter words can understand
That's why Ninnyhammer wept like a scatological hair-brain
When Com bent the knee & asked for hammy's hand

Some called their union cockalorum and fopdoodle fudger
But I gnashgab at how they're all so snollygoster cruel
It was obvious when they first discussed ultracrepidarian pap
There's was a love straight out of old snecklifter school

So spare a thought for highly sexed clinomanical adjectives
Who just want to get their contumelious dictionaries on
Life is too short for short words, said a smitten Ninnyhammer
As they ran off into the nonsensical sunset, wordy gone...

ROOSTER OUTSIDE THE HEN HOUSE

Here lie the battered remains of the almost infamous Mark Barry
A scandalously talented individual who almost succeeded
He almost got on the best sellers list and saw his work in movies
But there was always another path more urgently needed

He had hoped that his demise would make his writing soar in value
At fevered auctions for outrageous sums of mullah indecent
But he wasn't gay or bi or trans or even a cross dresser of real note
He got the occasional offer but was disappointingly decent

MB wished you'd buy property, fuck fear and look after your teeth
Although poor Baz had neither a lottery win nor a pot to piss in
But he was very good at saying big words that meant bigger things
Like, how can life be finished when you're still waiting to begin?

His ragged genius was admittedly something of an acquired taste
And some claimed they'd seen better copy on a cereal box
But he remained hopeful of one more strut outside the hen house
Rooster still crowing at the prize, final rock out with the cocks...

WAH WAH WAH
(Golden Years)

What is life? What is remembered? What is forgotten with cruel time?
Our passage on this crock of contradiction dissipates fast
The music I love is over 50, 60, 70 years old and travelling backwards
In a decade, I'll pushing up daisies with singers of the past

Rock and Roll will never die – Soul Music will go on being cool forever
Every genius and their legacy, every Genre, will never fade
But there's i-Phones documenting an abandoned chateau in France
Trampling over glory, swiping cobwebs, façades decayed

We seek out inspiration and sustenance from the feisty Golden Years
On a stage where even the most extraordinary light recedes
So, I play the songs and albums that keep me tingling and motivated
And smile at my poster of David Bowie, rocking stellar deeds...

For 'The Thin White Duke'

EMPEROR PALPATINE'S SKIN-MOISTURIZING TECHNIQUES

Emperor Palpatine's Skin Moisturizing Techniques is my favourite book
Went to Number 1 on the Health And Happiness Guru charts
Second only to *Benny Hill's Halitosis Tips For Chasing Girls Around Trees*
And that stunner, *King Kong's Repair Guide For Biplane Parts*

Proportional Dynamiting of US Mail Trains by Butch Cassidy is a blaster
I ate up *Fire Extinguisher Brands You Need To Avoid* by Jaws
Sports Bra-Fitting For Megalomaniacs with Three Nipples by ES Blofeld
Gave my undergarments regimen a definite cause to pause

And who can forget *Luke Skywalker's Guide to Surviving Daddy Issues*
Or *Cleopatra and Marc Anthony Quietly Toss Caesar's Salad*
I've dog-eared my *Travis Bickle's Successful Handbook to Taxi Driving*
Cherished my *Joker's Face-Painting Classes with Sulfuric Acid*

Removing Difficult Stains On Hand Towels by a blameless Pontius Pilate
Was also a huge smash with Jimmy Saville, working at the BBC
He read *Effective Lollipops* by Chitty Chitty Bang Bang's Child Catcher
Sent a copy to Prince Andrew, honourable as Jeffrey E in NYC

Getting The Most Out Of Sunblock by Icarus has always been a sizzler
Is almost as good as *Finding A Faithful Wife* by Henry the VIII
But my all-time upsetter is *Panting and Panties* by leggy Sharon Stone
Liable to make my basic instinct hard and nutsack palpitate

Life would be dull without cinematic pyro-techniques/gross-out laughs
Kenneth Williams crying *Infamy!* In the brilliant *Carry On Cleo*
And huzza for *007's Best Ever Magnets For Removing Women's Zippers*
Running Up Walls In Crotch Tight Leather by The Matrix's Neo

So here's to the Chippendale's buff masterwork *The Buns of Navarone*
And the BBC's woke cooking epic - *Sex, Lies and Garlic Bread*
And *Running Up That Stranger Things Hill* with Kate's Upside Down Bush
As *Capt. Kirk's* Phaser gives his Spock, some enterprising head...

LOST THE PLOT

I dated Little Bo Peep for a month of Sundays
But she wouldn't put out, no matter what
I rang up Jack Horner in his concentric corner
But the mention of Bo and he lost the plot

Poor Humpty Dumpty is incommunicado too
Moon Cow denying him his conjugations
Big Bad Wolf has implored The Ministry of Sex
A lack of Red Riding, unite all the Nations

But I had no such problems with Lady Godiva
Who dismounted her horse to man-hump
We went dogging with Robin Hood of Loxley
Although that Friar Tuck was a heffalump

But Godiva then decided to taste adventure
Try out one racier extra-curricular activity
She broke off the car aerial from her Cortina
And started to whip my Mowgli with glee

I went to the Fairy Tale Characters Sex Clinic
Because my Prince Charming was green
Tinker Bell screamed that's the worst case of
Van Aerial Disease I've ever fuckin seen!

SQUEEZING OUT SPARKS
WITH GRAHAM PARKER IN STOCKHOLM

I'll never forget when Rolf Borg (yes that surname) assured me
The train into *Stockholm* would arrive at precisely 10:23
He'd holidayed in Dublin and met his bride (my friend) Angela
But he also knew that Irish transport was cack (tee hee)

So I stood on the *Järfälla* platform and sure as God made poo
In rolls the stock, doors open, punters exit; new ones in
So we're heading into Sweden's capitol city on 7 August 1979
I even see half of Abba in a Volvo, fat chauffeur's grin

Slowing for the next stop, he points to a broken platform clock
And smiles; will be fixed this afternoon when we return
And as sure as Satan made the flimsy roof to contain the khazi
Later it functioned correctly, harmonious hours to burn

Even back then, Swedes paid a boatload more personal taxes
A Socialist Government repaying with logjams cleared
But I found it all clinical and detached and just so fucking cold
I longed for my Dublin where actual efficiency is weird

I was lucky to angle a ticket for Graham Parker and The Rumour
Stood there as his band debuted *Squeezing Out Sparks*
Thinking about the carved communal Chess Sets left out at night
They'd be petrol-doused in Dublin; toast in public parks

Over the decades I've recounted their staggering social services
How everything utilized their natural resources of wood
But I still can't decide if visitor-shoes-off for someone else's home
Is bollox or behavioural pointers that could do us good

So I think about all those gorgeous Master Race Swedish Blondes
Looking like Anni-Frid and Agnetha in Mamma Mia prime
And wonder why Irish Angela left Dirty Dublin for Spick Stockholm
When she could have had my ragged shamrock sublime...

For ANGELA and ROLF BORG and THE CHILDREN OF THE REVOLUTION

BENCHING BARRY WHITE
(Langers and Mash)

It's 1974 and *Be Thankful For What You Got* by William DeVaughn
Is played by the lurve-DJ - craftily slowing down the mood
You've summoned up Herculean courage, asked cutie to dance
Pulled her close, but *Langer Alert*, up pops something rude

Painfully aware of your involuntary macho libido in a public place
You panic as she chuckles, registering your motivated poke
The Saints of International Piety are demanding jail without parole
For your lack of propriety over that infernally excitable yoke

You hazard a kiss and find that's its bliss and suddenly you're hard
Where once in swimming pools, Percy was cruelly berated
Now the mere sight of a smock, Levi bum or lamb's wool tank top
And your once sedate Johnson, is most acutely stimulated

Soon you're all *Langers & Mash*, jumping up and down in car seats
Fumbling with bra-straps in a fleapit matinee showing Jaws
You've a stain on your corduroy that isn't a Cadbury's Fry's Crème
Where your faucet was encouraged to obey nature's laws

Several fathers have formed vigilante groups and flown out to Sicily
Where they were eagerly taught tooth and nail extractions
Next time you go near *their blemishless*, it won't be a horse's head
But something south of *your* border, ceasing all transactions

Flicking a wah-wah guitar, digging the scene with a gangster lean
Here comes another sister with her bellbottoms on just right
But who's that behind her with an axe and fourteen industrial pliers
Maybe I'll turn off the turntable - and *Bench My Barry White...*

AMBASSADOR TRIPLE BILL

The domed old-school *Ambassador Cinema* on O'Connell Street
Was the go-to fleapit of choice for cheap daytime-flicks
They'd cram the Balcony Area with budget-conscious Sci-Fi nuts
Carrying a Lord of the Rings paperback the size of bricks

So, we took our premium seats with Smarties Tubes and Popcorn
Guzzling a Jumbo Coke for the *Star Wars Triple Marathon*
Me with my brother Damien hoovering the original Lucas trilogy
Six hours of Skywalker and Vadar and the Jedi Obi-Wan

Those opening battleship sequences blew our tiny Dublin minds
Ludicrously creative edge-of-the-seat space opera shots
We'd drool at Princess Leia in a skimpy outfit, galactic negligee
While chomping down a Curly Wurly, chased by Jelly Tots

The loo became a pressing need half-way through *The Empire*
But it risked missing Lando Calrissian, a rogue striking back
So, you'd rush out during the miniscule interval curtain closures
Return to see our Millennium Falcon, or Death Star attack

How did we manage such enthusiasm and energy outpouring?
And why does it still exert such an intense pleasurable pull
Because we were family, doing what we loved to do together
Sat there in that fantasy, immersed, googly, our hearts full...

For my brother DAMIEN

PLAYING PATIENCE WITH THE BEATLES

To start my creative day, I play 'Patience With The Beatles'
Fifty-three card illustrations in the official Apple pack
And if I get out five descending sets of alternating colours
I'll hammer productivity on my ancient upstairs Mac

This ritualistic nonsense probably wouldn't pass any critique
As the Ace Of Spades turns over on 1970's *Let It Be*
But I love seeing *Revolver* show up on the King of Diamonds
Four of Hearts, live on the *Ed Sullivan Show*, US TV

King of Clubs has them walking across *Abbey Road* in 1969
With cryptic Volkswagen Beetle and a shoeless Paul
Queen Of Diamonds depicts a cherubic *Please Please Me*
Seven of Hearts *Magical Mystery Tour*, bus madrigal

Five of Spades has them wearing snow capes filming *Help!*
Ace of Diamonds, portraits from the *Double White*
Nine of Hearts has a bearded John walking Tittenhurst Park
About to spring a *Revolution* on *Hey Jude* tonight

The Queen of Clubs shows their mop-top haircuts circa '63
Seven of Diamonds has *Sgt. Peppers* Fixing A Hole
But of all the cards, I like the transition ones after *Yesterday*
Where they morphed into artists with *Rubber Soul*

I bought and sold their LPs and 45-Singles as part of my job
Twenty years filtering out their stunning catalogue
Greatness leaves a legacy that echoes across generations
The rest of us chasing the creative hair of the dog

Will we ever see their like again; know such musical genius?
When every release thrilled and properly amazed?
I don't know. But I'm a *Paperback Writer*; I'm working it out
Honing it, daily inspired by the artistry they blazed...

For JOHN, PAUL, GEORGE and RINGO
And their astonishing legacy of joy

VALENTINE'S DAY
(When I'm 66, Never Mind 64)

It's a good Valentine's day if we don't club each other to death
Maybe get the recycle bins of plastic and bottles out on time
It's a romantic afternoon when we duck at that flying frying pan
Watch the ooze of brains mix favourably with grease & grime

It's a marvellous celebration if we make it out of IKEA's spaghetti
With our wallets, brains, and nervous systems generally intact
It's a lovely sight to see when a weak bladder and sciatica nerve
All function relatively well, look forward to lasering a cataract

Can't wait to kiss you luv, but I must find my teeth and Steradent
And make sure the catfood bowl in the kitchen doesn't pong
We can make love over the washing machine like they do in films
Provided the delicate whites and soft linen cycle isn't too long

Later we can share a candlelit dinner by the used Zimmer Frames
Scoff down 2 Low-Fat Sugar Free Weight Appropriate desserts
Hold each other's genitalia for a period of more than one minute
And see if anything arises, coagulates or possibly even squirts

But as you smile in the kitchen, and we giggle over a hearty meal
And the day winds down with tele, books and Net trawling
I'm always going to be the one who races to open a door for you
And like Tom Waits sings, in my Sunday Best, come calling…

AWKWARD REACH

On the lurid surface, Britney Spears is just another wastrel Popster
Who doesn't warrant such ludicrous publicity or care?
But on closer examination of her totally controlled incarceration
We find manipulative Daddykins, working her despair

But a movement got going, holding up message-word placards
Have been working the public's short span of attention
Screaming like hurt children for Spear's legalese conservatorship
To end after 14 years of enforced controlled detention

But I wonder why such a waspy girly singer and her car crash life
Should elicit such a frenzied public outpour of emotion?
Clutching their radios in awe as she testifies in a macho US court
Her crew shivering in total allegiance and fan devotion

Is it that deep down inside all of us, lurks the secret terror thought
That we too are subjected to a reign of controlling ties?
Are we all just well-trained easy-to-shape lemmings marching to
Jackboots: to someone else's cleverly constructed lies?

Having power over your personal life, choices, finances and kids
And to monetize it, is a legally horrific freedom breach
So, I wish the lady singer fresh growing up years with her children
And God Bless *All Protestors* and their *Awkward Reach*...

For BRITNEY SPEARS and her carers

DESK CLERK DRESSED IN BLACK

"Hail! Hail! Rock and Roll! Deliver me from the days of old!"
Chuck Berry sang on Chess Records, all was saved
But it was the King who rescued us from decorous dances
His "Heartbreak Hotel", all gyrating and depraved

I framed the 78" for HMV POP 182 in its gorgeous label bag
Protecting the British ten-inch shellac disc, so brittle
My "All Shook Up", "Hound Dog" and "Blue Suede Shoes"
Have pride of place on my wall too, lick and spittle

Keith Mowser was a customer of mine at Reckless Records
Remembered hearing Elvis Presley conquer his street
A pal of his had the record and was blasting its dark magic
Out through the window directly to his post-war feet

Keith's face always filled up with joyousness at the thought
Of that stunning sound; been solid gone ever since
Suddenly everything seemed possible in his drainpipe work
A Rock 'n' Roll record made every pauper a Prince

In 1956 we were all from a musical town called Squaresville
It was a sharp right turn, heading south of Hick City
Where freckles, Lawrence Welk Waltzes and flat Crew Cuts
Were deemed to be wholesome, polite and pretty

Protect us Lord from Great Balls of Fire and A-Wop Bopping
And Three Steps To Heaven charting their mortal sin
Establishment blew a gasket when Rock & Roll bust through
And suddenly it was us and not them that could win

So here's to the King of Rock & Roll who saved the teenager
From the tyranny of narrow-minded musical cack
Because every time I eye those framed HMV 78's on my wall
I ache with pride at <u>our</u> desk clerk dressed in black...

For ELVIS PRESLEY who saved us all (and fan KEITH MOWSER)

HAND TOWELS FOR PONTIUS PILATE
(An Unholy Mess)

Dear Moronicus, I'm writing to you as a fellow Roman judicator
I keep dreaming of J Caesar and The Ides of March
And I've had Hellish problems with my post-orgy toga laundries
Probably vinegar mixed in with their Christian starch

You've probably seen my previous requests for 30 hand towels
And enclosed are pieces of silver to match that fee
You see, ever since I absolved myself of that Galilean prophet
They seem to pass on every *I'm God* agitator to me

Uncorrupted and nice, I came to Judaea for Emperor Tiberius
Maybe trade with Pharisee crooks, sleep with slaves
But all I get to do is sentence to crucifixion braggers like *Jesus*
Who now says he'll soon be sauntering out of graves

And credit where it's due, apparently, he's doing big miracles
On lepers, whores, and other marginal taxation bands
But I must confess Moron that although I scrub with oil all night
I can't seem to purge this *reddish hue* inking my hands

So, if you can stop mosaic-making and eating grapes for a mo
Please send fresh linen to the enclosed heretic address
Because I swear to the almighty Zeus, I've rubbed my skin raw
But can't seem to rinse out these stains; *this unholy mess...*

CACKLING OVER CAULDRONS

As Samson juggled pillars, Delilah sighed at her bowl of Philistine Grapes
All moody about jewels and Israelites and having so little to wear
She fluttered her eyebrows at his manly torso, then saucily commented
A political situation arises every time I stroke your loincloth or hair

Robin Hood sat Maid Marion on his lap as they rode tandem horseback
She commented on his fabulous tights and pointed arrows a-quiver
Robin of Loxley smiled and said that her ample uppercut assets enticed
His Sherwood Forest hardwood to dismount, then stand and deliver

Napoleon quaffed down another croissant as Josephine bathed in milk
Then checked his watch to see when the invasion of Russia started
But when Josephine exited the solid gold bathtub all lactating-dripping
Napoleon and his motivated French imperial got very Bona-parted

When Old Nick was stopped by Paparazzi in Hell exiting a Girly Rehab
He'd been making mix-tapes, drinking heavily, his palms in a lather
When asked why women left him reciting verse at the gates of Hades
He cried out for Momma, but she was torturing his unfaithful father

Old Blues singers used to moan about their ladies mistreatin' 'n cussin'
As they stood cackling over cauldrons, studying evil all the time
But then they'd shimmy across the floor or saunter past on the streets
And nothing can save us; gorgeous allure, curvaceous sublime...

THE BLESSED EDDIE

We take things for granted in the access-all-areas Internet Age
Get blasé about innovators, the game-changers for real
I can remember when *Eddie Van Halen* first happened in Rock
Most guitar-players dropped down to genuflect & kneel

I wrote lyrics for a band in Dublin, called him *The Blessed Eddie*
And we worshipped at the altar of those first two WB LPs
Our jaw dropped to the floor at the cool riffs and hammer-ons
A staggering musicality beneath his technical expertise

By the time they got to album number six and flash MTV videos
Van Halen was one of the famous axemen anywhere
A solo flourish in the magical *Back To The Future* movie in 1985
Cemented his legend, but also brought fame despair

Citing inevitable differences, he left his Dutch namesake band
As his physical health deteriorated & medicines failed
But when he passed Oct 2020 from cancer, and aged only 65
Millions were genuinely destroyed, his genius derailed

But I always return to *Panama, Little Guitars* & *Hot For Teacher*
To get my shot of pyrotechnics and hairy Eighties fun
And smile like a teen with a brand new chew toy called *God*
When I listen to The Blessed Eddie prove, he was <u>one</u>....

For EDDIE VAN HALEN ad all our Guitar Heroes

INITIALLED POCKET MIRROR
(Good News For All Men)

We will not remember Mark Barry for his towering temerity
Or his relentless pursuit of understanding and respect
But instead ponder on his scurrilously bulging trouser area
Where his sausage was historically a criminal suspect

He tried to be humble according to his diary *Mr Condom*
But when he looked in a mirror was always overcome
He'd consumed four lorry loads of Max-Strength Ugly Pills
To reduce the impact of his rock-hard abs and bum

Verbose, loquacious, orotund and garrulous are not words
Many will experience in his agreeably libidinous writs
Too bogged down with the atrocious burden of greatness
Smothering in literary genius and massive silicone tits

But when his women began getting alarmingly cognisant
Giving his superior grey matter all sorts of lip and guff
He wrote to the Prime Minister warning of societal bedlam
When modern ladies all start *thinking and doing stuff*

So, at his memorial service with its gold hearse of Satinella
Mr. Mark did not fret from which afterlife-grail he'd sup
At the Pearly Gates, he popped his *Initialled Pocket Mirror*
And his humble visage immediately cheered Bazza up...

A FAILED PYROMANIAC CURSES ANTS

The symmetrical beauty of a fat box of Swan Matches
Followed by the yellow orgasm of bursting flame
Ever since I stopped being Teenage Mark Pyromaniac
My flamin' life has never been the flamin' same

When we were kids, we just wanted to set fire to stuff
Post-box slits and neighbour's creosoted fences
Any chance to blow shit up with two copper bombs
Felt like a Sherbet Fountain sizzler on the senses

We bought cap guns, sparklers and boxes of bangers
Emulating gunpowder nutters of Historical yore
When we'd finished terrifying strays and shopkeepers
We'd leg it to Moore St. and buy us some more

But my path as a manically giggling Mozart-ish arsonist
Was cruelly stopped by a conscience one day
While I was frying a Dublin ant with a magnifying glass
I got soppy and let the squirt skedaddle away

Now the smell of sulphur is limited to our wood-burner
And Paraffin to soaked white-firelighter-squares
I long for the simplicity of torching municipal buildings
Singeing my newly minted tussock of pubic hairs

But alas my would-be life of *Sergeant Major Firestarter*
Has evaporated like a cigarette packet warning
But there's still days when I hunker shirtless by my Huey
And dream of Napalm, *so fragrant* in the morning...

I'VE NEVER SLEPT WITH HARVEY WEINSTEIN THOUGH GOD KNOWS I'VE TRIED
(In the Dock with a Hollywood A-Lister)

When I stepped out of the lift your honour, it was two a.m.
And Harvey was in a bathrobe, inviting me inside
I thought it was about a part in a life-changing film project
Acknowledge my talents with his big manly pride

When he assured me that this *was* the auditioning process
I remembered my friends said, fealty seals the deal
I'd heard of Hollywood hypocrisy amongst moguls for sure
But I was young, and his interest in me seemed real

So I came along this afternoon your honour to help clarify
Be at one with my wronged co-workers in 'MeToo'
Yes there's a crew recording my admirable benevolence
A hairdresser, lifestyle coach and Vegetarian Guru

Sat at home during the worldwide pandemic your honour
I took a year off to read scripts, latte denial crazed
I knew that none of the bigger interviewers or TV channels
Would question my nurse betrayal, $$s never raised

You see they love me no matter what! I couldn't care less!
I can literally get away with murder! They appease!
It's repeated in England, Europe, Asia, Japan and Australia
Won't rock the boat with ratings, nor fame displease

But regarding Harvey Weinstein your honour, I must divulge
I heard nothing for years about his sickening dupes
It was someone else's fault you see and we remain chaste
That's the line given by all the rich and famous troops

Years later, I was on the red carpet in a revealing plunger
I didn't mind standing by him when statues lay within
"I've never slept with Harvey Weinstein your honour, oh no
I'm just here researching a role, *one I deserve to win...*"

MARTYRED FOREVER
(Chide Abide)

Like the next man, I admire a person with spunk and mettle
Willing to go ten rounds with doubt, proper bellicose
But there's another part of me knows that unless you curve
Fill relationships with compromise; loneliness is close

You've got to chide abide, take the taunts and slag drags
Though seething with rage, will yourself to *mediate*
Keep the flame alive by middle-ground/accommodating
Longevity and happiness require a lot of sublimate

We sling grappling hooks on the ramparts of relationships
Making our dictatorial and emotionally rigid stand
Vow to surrender no further love to this latest soul partner
Stomp off into alone, leading your marching band

Stuck in your craw, can't be the real deal, sold out myself
All these textbook thoughts cajole and sucker clever
But there is no one who hasn't thrown the first angry stone
And wished its ripple effect hadn't *martyred forever*...

BOBSLED SKID MARKS
(One Good Run)

I can vividly remember when meeting a woman was no bother
Connection to another lady not considered some big deal
The laughter in the canteen at midday, boozer come evening
Simply an older version of young teenage crush and squeal

And while none of us boyos was James Bond 007 Secret Agent
Winking at luscious with an olive Martini; shaken, not stirred
There wasn't the isolated disconnect of computing from home
Where you don't have to dress up, any real effort, deferred

Relationships came and went, straight back to the Hurt Locker
Picked up your battered heart and innards, dived in again
Tried to learn some lessons, but of course you failed to correct
Bobsled downward momentum, mistakes, skid-marks, stain

Survival thinking remembers the good hook-ups and successes
And not the lonelier nights listening to poor-me vinyl songs
But I can also remember being of the absolute belief, prepped
One good run, up ahead, would right all the other wrongs

When you look back through the sober prism of time-a-fleeting
You wonder what would have happened, different route
And you shudder at that naïve young man hurtling through life
Never met that partner, children, donned a wedding suit…

KEEP IT RIGHT THERE Y'ALL
(Average White Boys)

When I reminisce on sweaty nightclubs and megawatt speakers
Keeping it right there y'all as we hit the floor to dance
I recall some seriously tortured moves masquerading as stepping
Heaps of us white R&B lovers shaking ants in our pants

We'd boogie all night to Earth, Wind And Fire, Chaka and Prince
Twelve-Inch singles extending the Nile Rodgers groove
Flaying beats until we dropped, our hips contorted, dogs barking
Trying to woo a girl with your Average White Boy move

But there's nothing dismissible about the Soul and Funk we loved
The 70ts & 80ts sound, still the staple of many FM stations
Will we ever see another Motown, Stax, Atlantic; Warner Brothers
All those fabulous songs, messages, uptempo creations

Maybe we are old and in the way, should bugger off, move it on
Stick old Aretha Franklin, Bill Withers and Stevie Wonder
But I'm never going to stop listening to their fantastic Soul legacy
Marvin's sexy genius, stirring up the rhythm down under...

For SOUL BOYS and GIRLS and DANCERS everywhere

BIG STRONG TOYS
(For Big Strong Boys)

Because he did the advert for the *Milky Bar Kid* on Irish tele
Seamus O'Rourke was always flush with the greens
Which meant, whilst we'd piddly Woolworths pistols & caps
He'd a *Johnny Seven O.M.A.* designed by marines

From bi-pod legs, the One-Man-Army threw hand-grenades
And clearly cost his one-upmanship folks a packet
With seven gun-slots, twelve rubber bullets and massive box
Next to our sulphur poofs, it made a serious racket

But his comeuppance came from an Orange Dumper Truck
Its mighty metal frame made of sterner *TONKA* stuff
"Big strong toys for big strong boys…" their adverts seduced
And for 1970s indestructibility, I couldn't get enough

Years later, we'd meet in Castilla Park with vinyl under arms
And laugh at what was once so sacrosanct for kids
Agree that most of Action Man's extravaganza weaponry
Probably puckered up both our parents dustbin lids

It was never about whose toys were better value for money
Was always ENORMITY got us ego-mutts deranged
And when we grew up, working in offices and boardrooms
TONKA spirit survived, because nothing's changed…

THAT SLY DARKNESS
(Beating Captain Neg)

We're all on a formation journey spanning decades
With our fear dry-humping every emotional leg
But it's survival-important to remember to embrace
A strategy to scupper the slide of Captain Neg

Facing up to the daily blunt trauma of the real world
Is fraught with all manner of invitational triggers
Yet even though it *feels like* your losing crucial battles
There are ways to beat its sly darkness sniggers

Constantly reinforce yourself with the proven mantra
Should racing thoughts begin their crafty fuss
What you feel is uncomfortable, not life-threatening
Panic attacks subside; they're not dangerous

This simplistic code may come across as an exercise
In glib phraseology, smacks of magazine pout
But its life-saving abilities have to be practiced hard
Drummed into thoughts pre-set to auto doubt

It's uncomfortable, but it isn't dangerous is your key
A technique that suppresses the panic attack
You don't rid yourself of its symptoms, but you cope
The next time that mind trickster sashays back

You may convince yourself that today is penultimate
But remember the darkness said that before
And you didn't die; you didn't implode or evaporate
You got through it, not beaten, here, *secure*...

For our daughter JULIA HOPE

LORD OF THE MINGS

Across the great transvergence and fissure of mythical time
Rode seven dark horses with their makeup and hair sublime
Behold the Mighty of Bosom and Hairy of Fan
Dorothia and Bustierre of the Minge Well Clan
To save Hobbits from the Dark Lord, *Hard On of Stiffy Climb*

With the sacred text of Sucky Fucky and the Sword of Dicky
They mounted Mordor's Mount Doom for a Gandalf quickie
Going down on Gollum and Sorcerer's brew
In fetching leather bondage of Legolas hue
They happily swallowed Two Towers of Orc love-spunk sticky

Dorothia did rimjob the Nutsack Rider of Back-Passage Way
While Bustierre shafted the Serpent of Schwarzenegger Bay
Neither entertained even a moment of flinch
Deep-throating Aragorn's Helm's Deep inch
While Gimli, Arwen and Boromir wrangled in threesome hay

Middle Earth warriors and hairy-footed men of Hobbit Lore
Pay attention as I sing of Fairies and Elvish gobbling galore
And fiery cauldrons with etched golden rings
With blowjob handshandy Lord Of The Mings
And be glad there aren't forty-seven million chapters more...

WE GOT YOUR BACK

I often wondered did you swim serenely in someone else
A globule inside another woman's tummy sublime
Later run towards your lover at a clock-dial's rendezvous
And launch into his arms, do the emotional climb

Did your briefly formed Ectopic Soul, relocate corporeal?
Fly away into another nurture vessel to be reborn
The one child we weren't allowed to bring up as a family
A life we never saw unfold, your story fabric torn

My first wife was *Jean*, a Northern Ireland Protestant lady
And we met again today 26-years after the event
We talked quietly about the saw-stab randomness of loss
Regrets of youthful inexperience, histories misspent

But today felt like an ending and even a second chance
Both feelings ping-ponging to & fro as we moved
Walking by the seawall with your long-time second hubby
My Mary Ann absent, closure moment approved

Neither of us focused on our respective partners or jabbed
Only what was lost all those painful decades ago
The private hurt we've both buried down deep about you
The family photographs not there, nothing to show

So you run wild and free our wee Ectopic Soul Boy of Love
We wish you only happiness & adventures galore
And as you navigate the bounty paths of life's possibilities
Remember, *we got your back* and so much more...

For JEAN DOOLE and our Lost One

YOSEMITE KEROSENE

Water-dropping helicopters along with 300-firefighters
Began tackling a raging wildfire in Yosemite Park
A giant mature sequoia is one of nature's tallest trees
Vulnerable to Nevada winds and Kerosene spark

There's a trunk amongst them called The Grizzly Giant
Estimated to be a staggering 3000-years of age
But it could be laid to waste by climate change amok
Aided by mankind's carelessness, centre stage

The nearby village of Wawona was evacuated of 600
Smoke and flame threatening, noxious nearby
But the campers cried for other reasons than blur eyes
All that nurturing beauty replaced, toxicity sky

They'll undoubtedly find the wanker and his cigarette
The lazy tourist disrespecting wondrous green
And when they do, I've asked for legacy punishment
Walk in the ashes of children; futures unseen...

For ENVIRONMENTALISTS Past, Present and Future

SHIFTY TUCO and the BULLETBELT BABES

We adored Pistolero Banditos and hotcha Bulletbelt Babes
Filling our Seventies teles, home from boring school
Linda Cristal was the Latino ranch wife to Big John Cannon
In TV's *High Chaparral,* made Irish buckaroos drool

Lee Merriweather then played Ann in Allen's *The Time Tunnel*
Julie Newmar wowed in *Catwoman*'s clingy leather
Fab Alexandra Bastedo in *The Champions, Avengers'* Emma
To Glynis Barber as *Dempsey's Makepeace* upsetter

Raquel Welch in *One Million Years BC* and *Fantastic Voyage*
Ursula Andress bikini-exiting the sea in Bond's *Dr. No*
Anita Ekberg in the *La Dolce Vita* fountain, wow Sophia Loren
Wearing anything, always had our loins good to go

Angela Sarafyan, Thandie Newton and Evan Rachel Wood
Provide the same in *Westworld*'s harsh fantasyland
Where Cowboys and Indians cannot wait to get all native
Give those paying customers a realistic robot hand

As the executioner reads out his long list of transgressions
Tuco looks shifty on a gallows, rope around his neck
Juan Ramirez (former known as The Rat) is *The Ugly One*
A Mexican brigand working a scam, soon to collect

Clint Eastwood plays *Blondie*, accurate with a Winchester
Chews half-lit cigar stumps; he badly needs a shave
While Lee Van Cleef plays *Angel Eyes*, a merciless *Baddie*
Looking for Bill Carson's $200,000 loot hid in a grave

But these Spaghetti Men are fodder once the ladies show
Loaded duds guaranteed to make all shooters bolster
Sexy Sharon Stone, Lucy Liu, Megan Fox and Salma Hayek
Haunting every young cowboy's trigger-happy holster...

WE LAUGH AT IT NOW

I once chased my younger sister Frances up the stairs
With a kitchen knife, as brothers are want to do
We'd had a teenybopper kerfuffle about Rock Songs
So she had to be terminated by you know who

Though it seemed like perfectly reasonable behaviour
At the time (an appropriate harmless response)
She took umbrage to my serrated blade-jab offensive
And called me a phrase not dissimilar to nonce

Three decades later, reminiscing as sibling grown-ups
We recalled other antics cutting a memory rug
And realised that what was once so damn important
Has become a future punchline, derisive shrug

We laugh at it now of course; even admire its passion
And children testify that Fran did indeed survive
Today I look with huge brotherly affection at my sisters
And thank blunt cutlery, that we're all still alive...

For FRANCES and CATHY

ROMEO REMOVAL PILL
(Where's Elon When You Need Him)

Relationship rejection inflicted on us in our teenager years
Returns in our dotage with undiminished power
When our heartache felt like a tornado-malicious sinkhole
Just hearing a love song could all hope devour

Adventurous youth populate TV Shows and hipster movies
Flitting from one loved-up wall-slam to another
The elasticated-heart dime-dropping undying devotionals
On the head of the latest more fanciable lover

Is it that our race has been run and our love number is up?
As we smile warm at other people's happiness
The years melting into wrinkles and routines and tablet vials
And bedrooms with little to celebrate/confess

The mistakes we made in love all those vivacious eons ago
Creep up on us in our unguarded moments still
So I keep watching pretty young things living their best lives
As I wait for Elon to invent a Romeo-removal pill...

SLITHERING IN MY ROOTS
(Rinsing Mr. Deflated)

Weary after another successful sortie into someone's psyche
Mr. Deflated checked into *The Double Negative Hotel*
He showered quickly - then exfoliated any pallor and residues
Of dead dreams, broken hearts and such like bagatelle

Took a motivational video by *Professor We're So Hard Done By*
Grateful for seven highly effective whinging techniques
Had breakfast with his mentor *Capt. Let's All Obfuscate Today*
Ordered up assassination attempts on 6 positivity freaks

His favourite Eighties band is *Frankie Goes Absolutely Nowhere*
And their seminal debut *Welcome To The Poo Poo Dome*
His preferred haunts are sweatboxes, latrines and a McDonalds
He'd buy a prison, but there's a tax on a second home

Mr. D. enjoyed the incarceration flick *The Fuck All Redemption*
As a tunnel of shit almost asphyxiates Andy DuFresne
But he intensely disliked the upbeat ending about a new start
And there needed to be far more *no hopers* in frame

Mr. Deflated has signed up to a lifetime membership for sloth
At his nightclub *That Chip On Your Shoulder Really Suits*
But I for one am considering getting me a professional haircut
Rinse out his despondent colours *a-slithering in my roots*...

YOU DON'T HAVE TO BE MAD TO WORK HERE

Preserving the past became a sort of religion for us in *Reckless*
Self-confessed vinyl junkies, foldout gatefold in hand
Buying and selling albums and singles and yer rob-wallet rarities
The must-have music from your chosen artist or band

I'd kerfuffle in front of Terry O'Sullivan's *Loricraft Audio PRC 6*
A hand-built professional record-cleaning machine
Listen to the thread play the music while it sucked up gunge
Revitalising the grooves of another curvy evergreen

We'd open at ten, close at seven, the sounds never stopped
Cram a shuffle-play with every possible genre need
The jokes would fly around as you served the religious faithful
Double-check grades, artwork, label's up to speed

You'd still get a thrill from those 60ts and 70ts laminate sleeves
Genuflecting in front of legends, assuming position
But as the decades marched on, what was once so plentiful
Became so difficult to get in a playable condition

After 20-years of buying and selling huge collections of worth
I swung a heart-attack at 54 and never did recover
I've still got the RR Neon from the window of 30 Berwick Street
The shop that's featured on the Oasis *Story* LP cover

But my fondest memories are of me with the boys and the gals
Shooting the spit about albums that really mattered
And the thrill of finding that rarity you'd been lusting after yonks
Before we lost Peel and our teenage kicks shattered

Too many of our musical heroes are now shedding mortal coils
And it's a process that sadly goes on now, unabated
So I crank up the amp, lift up the Perspex lid, talcum on the lino
And *Get Back* to *What's Going On*, my *Soul* elevated…

For all the STAFF and CUSTOMERS bought from and sold to
At *RECKLESS RECORDS* in London's ISLINGTON and SOHO

PARADISE PRONOUNED
(Cancel Culture)

The Catholic Church has been forced to refurbish Purgatory
Due to an unprecedented influx of Venial Sin
The overseeing committee for Shitheads and Semi-Fuckwits
Decides who gets excluded and who gets in

Lucifer, however, is arguing parameters for greed and vice
And is unhappy at their pronoun interpretations
He maintains that in order to be a proper cunt in UK politics
You should copy Nicola Sturgeon's inclinations

She leads the way in stabbing your former allies in the back
Then claiming you had no idea what was lost?
Flagellating Scottish Independence to death with bullwhips
Whilst secretly pissing your kilt at the fiscal cost

God has managed to remain a non-inclusive independent
And refuses to be drawn on such piddly things
It seems his gift of freewill to mankind continues to bugger
As we sabotage any Utopia the future brings

So maybe I won't listen to Talk Radio or surf a poisonous Net
Where society's know-it-all twats seem to lurk
Looking for some new angle to hang the *Cancel Culture* on
While the rest of us rise early and haul to work

Like radicalized Muslims, so many cults dictate sideways bile
As they battle it out for the jurisdiction of Souls
I long for a future where Gilead is named as freedom-ruinous
Just another book of male dominated controls

Paradise Pronouned/Segregated isn't anybody's truth, ever
Include instead, all of God's diverse creations
Because the more I witness how overlording enables haters
The more I'll crave, a life free of manipulations...

ROOM FOR THE FORSAKEN

Is there room for the forsaken on the last locomotive to Heaven?
Maybe redeem themselves by offering up their seats anew
Can anyone ride towards the light whose been squat in malaise
Left hope gathering shelf-dust, yellowed diary turning blue

Who in this world of twilight can honestly speak of taming regret
Watching the countryside fleet by on that last rolling stock
Thinking of loved ones waiting up ahead with canyon-sized arms
Dropkick deadwood, chuck away your past-tethered clock

I hope the station we arrive at is full of bustle, sawdust Tearooms
Tub Porters sorting repurposed luggage, piggledy stacking
Where the sun rises to the smell of buggies with burnished wood
Where all is possibility, connection; no traveller left lacking

Does an imperfect corporeal voyage really determine our sequel?
A life raked over by some judgemental halo-headed court
Because I look forward to a horizon navigated in weightlessness
Where no soul gets kiboshed, dreams never come up short…

BEEHIVE and BOUTONNIÈRE
(Crossing You In Style)

Jean Vera Wilson was our neighbour of some 30 years in E17
They shared 72 Penrhyn Avenue with four grown-up tots
Angela, Alan, Richard and youngest (budding writer) in Lucy
Council house, did the pools, garden of vegetable plots

Jean used to paint as a young woman in the Swinging Sixties
Sold her railing art on the Portobello Rd, groovy and hip
Married her beau to a backdrop of The Beatles & The Stones
Became a stay-at-home mum, tending to knee and lip

On her July 2022 memorial booklet is a small photo on the rear
Of a teenager stood outside the registry with a happy grin
Wedding her Carnation Buttonhole Ken in Lava Lamp clobber
She in her Dusty Springfield beehive hair, so fashionably in

But even when we moved into 70 Penrhyn Avenue in early 1991
Jean was frail from a lifetime addicted to filter-tip fags
She'd bake us hot apple pies that I swear channelled Rothmans
While I'd reciprocate by fixing their Internet & Tele snags

In the booklet there's another memory photo of a suited ladylike
About town in her Audrey Hepburn *Moon River* beguile
And that's how I think of Jean with a dapper boutonnière hubby
As they both relive glam lives, crossing that river in style…

For JEAN VERA WILSON, 5 March 1948 to 12 July 2022
Our Neighbour and Friend in Walthamstow, E17, London
Her husband KEN and Family too

SHARKSKIN WEAVE
(Old Order Got To Go)

Things were simpler in the past and lawlessness an urban myth
Is the mantra of every TV/Net philosopher, hip and astute
It was all double-breasted Sharkskin Suits, gent-tipping Fedoras
Neighbourly living in the ascendance, no trickster or brute

Perhaps it may have seemed that way on the buffed porches
Of white picket-fenced suburban palaces of moral clean
But legal banishment to asylums for unladylike insubordination
Was the reality of the undertow, *institutionalized* obscene

Women had no real say in the rose-tinted view of pearly-white
The viciousness of male laws hidden beneath fisted greys
Today you're encouraged to turn on yourself on palm laptops
Dance to puppeteers; sign up to vitriol and smug malaise

War, genocide, torture holds, walls to keep out dirty immigrants
Is the appalling track record of a corporate-bought *male*
Men may talk it up when it comes to embracing a better world
But give them power or office and *inaction* is their prevail

Be wary of the race to go backwards; a snake oil compromise
Tug that chain, the more retro-obsessed media becomes
Because if you're not careful to actually secure a lady's future
Then all you'll ever have is brush-offs, tables full of crumbs

Slick Willy may come on all smiling-beguiling at campaign time
But is that wolf ever going to produce the pro-lady goods
Because all I see are so many women sleep-walking to Gilead
While Rooster smirks in his immaculately *intransigent* duds

Instead of hankering after a compromised sepia-tinted mirage
We need to run towards a future that let's everyone grow
And as much as I love you ladies, stop being a sideline gullible
Don your power-suits, force legislation; *old order got to go...*

CLEAN SLATE
(I Bet Holly Rocks)

I Bet Holly Rocks, declares another chalked Margate graffiti
The lovely Holster sending Kent Boyo Hearts into a flutter
No doubt sashaying past the admiring beach-buffed bums
Like in her mouth, never been a trace of melting butter

Oh to be so young, a world of opportunity at your fingertips
Fuck-ups and dumb choices not yet part of life's profile
All breaking hearts and busting balls and weekend warriors
The charge of sheer bravado making this old man smile

I hope fab Holly finds love and happiness in her eventful life
Gets a shot at a legacy worthy of Wikipedia paragraphs
And in her dotage, finds that her larder of wonder memory
Still has kindness in it, friendship and maybe even laughs...

SWELLIGANT

Last night I dreamt I crept into bed with the most gorgeous young woman
She smiled as she lifted the sheets on her soft curvaceous flawless glory
Even as I wandered in and out of consciousness, I knew it was all a dream
And that come the morning, age and years would tell a different story

A week back a twenty-something couple of hipsters passed with a pooch
Maybe they will never have children or responsibility, be accident prone
And in their demeanour, I saw that devil-may-care-surety-cauldron gurgle
That makes them think they will never want for love, or end up, all alone

Lady Luck and her loaded dice is rarely a lingerie model scantily reclining
More likely to be a nurse swabbing bandages on your saw-crater chest
The days of you stopping cars, turning heads or wow-whistle caterwauling
Get replaced by blub belly and an unwillingness to ever get undressed

Life is an extraordinary crapshoot, ginormous ups and debilitating downs
Being in the right or the wrong place, determining horrible loss or gain
So may the glory of physicality and allure always rock your current world
Its long legs of promise like hope eternal, washing away reality's stain...

MATE'S RATES

Andrew has been appointed *Ambassador for Female Empowerment*
With rare appearances being tastefully unobtrusive and sparse
But when asked to address abuse in all British legality regarding rapes
Sources close to the Palace say - HRH disappeared up his arse

When Epstein boarded his private jet for another liaison in Lolita Land
He didn't seem remotely bothered by heavy political weather
Jeffrey just smiled, and wished his new British Royal buddy *all the best*
Although sadly for victims, his recall then disappeared forever

Archaic laws regarding women/children offer sly liberal interpretations
That suit abusers cruising canal boats in Richmond and Surrey
And I can imagine Jimmy Saville O.B.E. giggling in corridors of the BBC
Got an appointment at a Care Home, cigars in excited hurry

Where are decent politicians chasing down pigs, monsters and defilers?
Where is support for those fighting sickos outside schoolyard gates?
They must be holidaying too, like Epstein, Andrew and his pal Weinstein
Laughing off charges, stroking mobiles, cushty with powerful mates...

LOVE ISLAND: ANCIENT EGYPT
(A Rough Week)

Wednesday, 10:23 a.m. - Nefertiti and Anubis Bond Over Enid Blyton

"After a long day down in the dungeons extracting nails from thumbs
I like to relax with a good Murder Mystery mam" Anubis admitted
Nefertiti turned around from the world's biggest mirror made of Gold
And replied, "ENID BLYTON!" Anubis welled up, practically shitted

Friday, 11;08 a.m. - Anubis Cheats On Nefertiti With Her Cat

"...I saw her there! Salaciously rubbing suntan lotion into her feline coat!
Something *Titty Kat* knows brings out the Pussy in me!" Anubis cried
"I don't mind in the slightest, dear..." Nefertiti purred in a chilling riposte
Then cut off his balls, diced mog No.8 and pyramided the lot inside

Saturday, 1:37 p.m. - Anubis Mourned by Irate Body-Positive Fans

"I know he disembowelled women/children down in the dungeons
But I liked his fashion choices and cookery tips...", Slim the Slave
"That Nefertiti is a two-timing slag and megalomaniacal fat bitch!"
Said Anubis who recently contacted ITV from beyond the grave

Sunday, 5;04 p.m. - Nefertiti Opens Up About Elizabeth Taylor and Marriages And Gives Her First Candid Online Interview About Her Breakup With Anubis and How, Somehow, Neffy's Managed To Soldier On

"I guess you could say I acted impulsively when I cut his gonads off!
But I was provoked..." Graham Norton and Nefertiti share a nod
"So, like Liz Taylor, I bought bigger diamonds, got another husband
And had him pay for my seventy-nine augmentations to my bod!"

Graham smiles benevolently as the audience offers up wild applause
Nefertiti flutters her sprinkled eyelashes, looking boxing clever
"So, you see Graham! Even though I loved Anubis *for over four weeks!*
I bare him no ill will. (Smirks to the audience)
Locked in my pyramid, *forever and ever....*"

MIRRORBALLS and FRUITCAKE

The *Buxom Wench* and *Fiery Gypsy* are Women of Legend
That the puritanical hierarchy have always despised
Yet lust and libido in a man of any decade or background
Is seen as OK acceptable; not morally compromised

I recall the racy girls were always objects of teenage terror
Coursing through their lips, the ultimate jolt of power
They'd smirk and shimmy and sprinkle like a hung Mirrorball
Sending out shards of light, eradicating ditsy cower

Some were overly sexual while others had that subtle cool
An open blouse versus a suggestive soft underneath
They'd drive you crazy with desire as they acted innocent
Bathroom boys scrubbing expectant crooked teeth

Yet it is they that my affectionate memories most flock to
The staggering legacy of go-ladies with experience
Where being in their embrace and loving the exploration
Transformed us saplings in every conceivable sense

All our make-up defences thicken as the march hammers
But the lifeforce women exude remains intoxicating
As they smile at the sideways longing of baldy gentlemen
All those goofy featherbrains they had fun liberating

Sex will always be a commodity to some, others repulsed
An emotional jurisdiction they down-crush with piety
But I am always going to eye a Rubenesque dessert trolly
As the most glorious temptress for a fruitcake like me...

CALLING INTERPLANITARY DAFT

I'd like to thank bug-eyed aliens for travelling across the Universe
To look up Homo Sapiens and their multi-denominational asses
This seems a really good use of intergalactic space-time blobules
As they tell us telepathically to wank into long test tube glasses

But here's a thought to pass on to E.T. as he hovers over a clearing
Waiting for some U.S. Trucker to gawk up at his tractor beam
Maybe bring us the solution to our total environmental destruction
You fucking idiot, instead of lubing our plumbing with cream

It's bad enough that we're now being told, we're no longer alone
And that advanced technology has been reverse engineered
When I only just got over a colonic irrigation in a Margate hospital
Where my non-binary scrotum has been polished and smeared

So here's to the little green men and extra-terrestrial Zippity Do Dahs
May they travel to Europe next time at twice the speed of light
Because if anything comes near my backside in the next millennium
They had better prepare themselves for a backlog of Irish shite...

EMANCIPATED TRUPENNY BITS

In 1970, I wasn't concerned when women burnt their bras
Making wobbly what had once been stiffly contained
I was terrified about the New Decimalization changeover
Teacher quizzing Ready Reckoners, male eejits caned

But just as I waved the past goodbye, soaking up the new
Adios to my short trousers and popping postulant zits
I suddenly began to focus on loose fitted tie-dye Tee Shirts
Sporting newly emancipated undulant trupenny bits

But just as our fashion-conscious girls hit the hip boutiques
Labels with two currencies ramped up every price
So, they doubled-down to easy and less expensive clothes
Where the pert results were both uplifting and nice

And rumour had it that they'd often lose more than clobber
As they embraced the *free* in Rock's emerging sound
So, I remember with affection, not the florin, but swirling inks
Curves, a new currency; our jaws scraping the ground...

MUSTN'T GRUMBLE

For calling out his Government on asylum seeker policy
TV's Gary Lineker has been hounded and dogged
Horrified in Hackthorpe and apoplectic in Aberystwyth
Are beside themselves OBE wasn't publicly flogged

Frenchmen have been rioting for four days about age
Retirement date is pushed to 64 by a sly president
In the Netherlands farmers are being told to forfeit 50%
Of all land, replaced by mega-cities upward bent

In Canada, Truckers wages were stopped by intrusions
From an administration bulldozing popular dissent
Mustn't grumble used to be the mantra of old England
Yet I'd argue their collective bulldog needs a vent

Somebody's going to emergency, someone else to jail
Is a lyric in a Don Henley song about banker greed
But I fear that if we don't protest more, mobilise bodies
Then we'll lose a lot more than time, turf and seed...

LIAR SPIEL
(Vacant Plot)

I'm convinced that it's only women who will save our World
While *men in power* will guarantee its Hellish extinction
Politicians have zero track records on protecting or revering
Always short-changing them in no-change dereliction

I'm old enough to remember men's endless sworn promises
As they canvassed every demographic, hustling votes
Then once in office, how the cold familiar malaise returned
The unavailability for interview, lack of any fiscal notes

We're facing an environmental melt of biblical proportions
Because deaf rudderless buffoons have had the wheel
I can only hope that women will finally assert their influence
Future-proof potential lost; broker an exit strategy deal

There is a real difference between *men* and *men in power*
Shafting our planet to retain their lucrative official slot
I pray that smarter women will bench the next fork tongue
Lest all we're left with is *liar spiel*: Earth, a *vacant plot*...

TOMMY TRENCHANT and the ZEN ARCHER
(Real Goose Bumps)

People are not interested in you being/becoming successful
Let alone reaching for it as you properly should
And the closer you get to anything that might construe a win
Up pops their jealousy, deviousness underhood

There's a piano player in this hotel bar dressed in suave attire
Tinkering the ivories, popular songs known by all
But as Tommy Trenchant dials the mood down to easy inertia
You can tell he knows, manning a knockoff stall

Any former defiance/rebel-yell is now kept firmly in gob-stasis
Reality checked by a monthly stump up of rent
And although he didn't pen the songs, as he strokes the keys
He knows he's better than, dressage proficient

We do things we don't want to, hold down jobs that paralyze
Sap our energies and palsy-enfeeble our marrow
Hope one day we'll halter the quiver filled with our true selves
And unleash that long restrained personal arrow

Twenty-20's, I'll take my inspirations wherever I can find them
And not shoot any piano player stroking malaise
Ignore the pleasantries man and forgive imitation merchants
Concentrate hard on the music from better days

So as we wait for the Zen Archer to quench our dehydrations
With newly minted bottles of Cool Aid for chumps
Let's play original 45s and Vinyl LPs instead of MP3 on Spotify
And recall we once looked for _real_ goose bumps...

GENESIS GETS A RHYTHM SECTION

After two days of bonding in orchards and brush-beating-out snakes
Adam admitted that despite Eve's ticklish entry, Eden was good
But ever the argumentative interloper, Eve grimaced at his air guitar
And found his hands spent far too much time playing with wood

Eve immediately started in on the serious lack of decent shoe stores
And how the airy urinal facilities sure put the outdoors into pissing
But Adam was too busy noticing the improved extensions up above
Whilst being freaked out by the appendage below gone missing

Adam quite liked the plump lips and pert bottom as she directed him
To pay attention to the changes that were imminently pending
But he was too excited by the way her long hair draped on nudie bits
As she discussed kitchen units, all curvaceous and body bending

Eve explained that *The Fantastic Lesbian God* of *The All-Girls Universe*
Had decided to give poor pitiful Man a *Woman* to aid his choices
Adam clutched his wound as he stifled the first of many loud guffaws
Surely this arguably shapely gal is *mad* and not just hearing voices

Adam explained that *Man* is the Lead Singer in a Big Balls Rock Band
And that *Woman* must settle for seconds in their Musical Direction
But as she looked down as his helplessly apparent ardour, Eve smiled
Knowing that Adam was always going to want, *A Rhythm Section*...

RICH AND ROYAL HUE
(Tapestry)

When I was fifteen and doing the wild longhaired air guitar
To Deep Purple, Led Zeppelin and the Sabbath Black
What girls we actually talked to would gawk at us mid flow
With a piteous scowl, call that Funny Farm right back

Next day, they would arrive with a powerful Emo antidote
Carole King's "Tapestry", sort those Satanists right out
Soon we were listening to sensitive lady singer-songwriters
Learning about earth moving, hearts mucked about

We'd devour lyrics printed in tufts on the single sleeve rear
Expressing the desires and longings of womanly lore
Maybe even sing about love's pallet of rich and royal hue
Instead of riffing Hobbits and Goblins and ritual gore

It was all very emotional and confusing for us young boys
Never did quite get their hurt profound, deepest grief
But we knew their eyes would light up at Joni and Carole
They'd found their mentor, hero valve; lifelong belief...

ALWAYS THE WAITRESSES

It was always the waitresses, apron-clad and swivel of hip
Alight on your table, pert and perky, mysteriously swift
Universal rule, they'd be a gorgeous student or Euro type
Impossibly sexy, booties, a tight blouse with bosom lift

They'd hand you menus mankier than teenage thoughts
And stand there pretend-smiling, but terminally bored
You'd order something Dublin-predictable like Ham Pizza
Or the Hamburger Special on the menu, underscored

They'd snatch the menus away from your best flirtatious
Smile and head back towards the hatch with a neon
You'd try to look unaffected by such illusive temptresses
But restraint is lost, sap breathless, head already gone

An appalling table service, twenty or thirty long minutes
Did little to diminish her arm-laden fantabulous return
You'd praise her handling of the physically challenging
Manoeuvres, she'd feign thanks, but advances spurn

You'd smile again as you left, as if she had noticed you
But she'd be chatting to her mates, placing hairclips
They'd be talking about travelling around rural Ireland
Ignoring every man Jack in the place, counting tips

I remember being amazed when I got to live in London
That every waitress working there was just the same
And even though the young ones acted all nonchalant
Their faces fell too, when beautiful exited the game

Housewives, pilots, nurses, actresses, Rock n Roll Singers
Architects, web designers, politicians, biologists too
But oh the glory when they shimmered in the headlights
Cast their spell; made mental mincemeat out of you…

MOMMY DEAREST
(Gateaux Sponges and Rock Buns)

Mothers will meddle and tamper with relationships
No one is ever good enough for their fruit
They carried you for almost a year of nipple torture
Then wiped the base of your birthday suit

Jack drinks like a fish and farts like Blazing Saddles
He's not a good fit for her daughter Niamh
And that knob Michael has a permanent erection
With packets of Super Trojans up his sleeve

Sharon has nothing in common with gobshite Dave
Except maybe they're spliffing in cahoots
Up in Sharon's boudoir with Pink Floyd on the stereo
Him in a cheesecloth shirt and Jesus boots

The doctors have poor Maeve on tranquiliser shots
Designed to curb her amorous appetites
But she keeps bringing home the entire office pool
Showing the lads entry holes in her tights

Mama has prematurely gone dolally in her dotage
And her waist adores them creamy cakes
But she'll not settle until her nippers are also settled
With partners who aren't cheap or snakes

Mothers may meddle and tamper with relationships
But she's only doing what she thinks is best
She'll give the Gateaux Sponges to Mr. & Mrs. Right
And gum-wrecking Rock Buns to all the rest...

THE CORRECT OPINION

Women are all for equality
As long as they're getting their own way

They think equality between the sexes is a truly fantastic idea
In theory

However, as she heads you off by the front door
About to make a denim apparel purchase of dubious fashion cognisance

You will quickly find out that *the correct opinion*
Oddly enough equates to *her* opinion

The genuinely frustrating part for both duplicitous affidavit participants
Is that nine times out ten

She's always right
And you're always wrong…

MEL BROOKS and ANNE BANCROFT

Odds and Sods, Bits and Bobs, Beauty and the Beast even
Love has had its fair share of couples buck the trend
You take one misaligned eejit over here, ringer over there
And suddenly two rough peopleoids perfectly blend

"We started talking and we never stopped...", said Brooks
Describing his first meeting with Anne Bancroft in 1961
Rehearsing in the Ziegfeld Theatre on Broadway 54th Street
They exchanged a stage/seat joke, bond was begun

AB was already a star and MB, a struggling comedy writer
But Anne saw a *future* in the goofball yet erudite Mel
Using one of her hoop-earring as an improv wedding band
They married in City Hall, the NYC clerk lisped as well

Mel made *Twelve Chairs*, *The Producers* & *Blazing Saddles*
His Wild West film spoof and celebrated masterpiece
Bancroft won an Oscar, three BAFTAs, 2 Globes and Tonys
The triple-crown of acting, June 2005, rested in peace

The Jewish word for fate or destiny is *Kismet*, an Act of God
Where the stars align for those that aren't arrow norm
Loved each other for over forty-years of careers & cancer
Celebrated the highs, safe place in a fearsome storm

Aged 97, Melvin James Kaminsky (Mel Brooks) is still with us
A hero for all generations, the *Get Smart* creator loved
But I bet that deep down Mel longs for the arms of his lady
Smiling on that celestial stage, funny-peculiar beloved...

THE GREAT RESET

I've come to believe that children save us from ourselves
And most broheem need all the saving they can get
A man is essentially a self-serving accumulations creature
Until trickster Mother Nature turns on *The Great Reset*

You try to grasp the magnitude of what's tummy growing
As the building blocks assemble a unique next of kin
You inventory, attend the classes, prep the incoming nest
And hope that you'll pony up when the stabs begin

You're holding hands and bags and baby paraphernalia
As the attending work whilst keeping the vessel calm
You're encouraging and positive-talking about breathing
When your knowledge of such pain/terror is a sham

There's blood and sputum and sweat and powerful drugs
As the screaming crescendos into a miracle wiggle
You're too relieved to feel the elation, blunt force wonder
As the triptych becomes one, tear-gush and giggle

You walk out of hospital and start to clock subtle hazards
Like vans parked too tight, cars hurtling by at speed
The Universe suddenly sending you pay-attention triggers
Where something vulnerable will succumb to bleed

We're parents now, invades your every fractious thought
Child becomes a man transition-phase just got real
100 calls, cards, congratulations, balloons and fluffy toys
Everyone coos the emotional jackpot, biggest deal

In the end, you sense that you've changed for the better
Maybe even got to patch over every previous flaw
But mostly, you never forget that arrival, our tiny beautiful
And all you could do was beam at your lady in awe…

SKYWARD
(Two Made It Through)

On the 20th of October 2006 at *The Forest Suite in The Old Vicarage*
Mark Barry and Mary Ann Simmons married with three in tow
Both 48-years *youngish* with our siblings of fifteen, twelve and eight
London E17 Walthamstow Registry Office, finally good to go

Our beautiful children Dean, Julia Hope and Sean all looked dazed
While work colleagues and friends sported a knowing smile
We'd been through enough to understand the You/I commitment
A together family, not wannabes, doing the long-haul mile

Our Dino looked awkward posing for our home wedding reception
Eager to get away from the body tsunami and music jams
Made a hasty exit to his Video and DVD player loftroom sanctuary
Away from the suited congratulating us middle-aged hams

But of all the shots our pal Niamh captured on that momentous day
There's one of my sister Frances dancing like Baloo the Bear
She knows her big brother has finally managed an inspired decision
A typically generous joy and delight in her giddy face stare

The cakes and the dips and the bowling alley row of exotic bottles
Hid a failed first marriage, similar relationships under the bus
But looking back at the photos of revellers having a genuine holler
I now know why Franny celebrated with such force and fuss

Second-chance Saloon is a destination some of us may never see
Formerly grounded pair get another go as a reinstated crew
And now I see it, behind Frances was my lovely Mary Ann, all lit up
Exploding like New Year's Eve. Skyward, *two made it through…*

NOT BODGING THE BIG STUFF
(Swimming Towards The Save)

When I think about the batshit things we delinquents did growing up
I'm amazed we made it out of our teens with *any* limbs intact
Nowadays its's all MRI Prostate Scans and aiming kaleidoscopic pee
Slice and Dice will cut me a good deal removing a cataract

Our poor ignorant parents had no idea about the booze and drugs
Or the laughing schoolgirls who eyed us with smart suspicion
We'd be giggling fortnightly in confessionals forced on us by priests
Making up lesser mortal sins, got us minimal acts of contrition

Copper bombs, playing in ruins, balancing atop footloose ramparts
Paralytic drunk in front of oncoming traffic, puking in hedges
Wake on someone's floor mattress, late for your repulsive office job
Aspirin the banging head, line the tum with toasted wedges

Physical injury or worse was probably stalking our every mad move
We just didn't seem to notice it, nor care us a fiddler's lament
Now in your dotage, all the unhealthy crud and long-finger choices
Haunts you as every manner of orifice gets buckled and bent

What was it benevolently watching over some of us and not the rest
Who decides if you go to the sharks or swim towards the save
Knew too many who didn't surface from the shenanigans and hijinks
Went into squats, doorways, down a path of the horror crave

No one in their thirties or forties actively considers failure up ahead
The hungry hubris of young-thinking still guaranteeing otherwise
But when you get to mid-term and great artistic success still eludes
There's a danger you view everything else as lame compromise

Takes a lifetime accumulating any wisdom on how to live properly
Balance the need to reach for wonder whilst gripping ground
To finally arrive at a place where your car tyres no longer screech
Where the hum of existence has a more mature kind of sound

I don't remember feeling then like we were in any form of danger
But I do remember emerging into my Sixties, a bullet dodged
And now that we face down a tumble into *Seventy Years of Age*
I give thanks for children, love, wife; *the big stuff not bodged...*

LOVE CANNOT WAIT
(The Wonder of Men – Part 122)

I love you my darling
And you love me
We love each other to bits

Which is why, when we argue
I cannot wait my dear
To get on your tits...

SHARP INHALE - INDEX
(Poem Titles in Alphabetical Order)

ABBY SUX FARTS (For Real Man) – Page 19
AFTER HER (Strange Magic Lurching Over Me) – Page 10
ALL THAT I STOLE (I Wish I Could Give It Back) – Page 52
ALREADY TAKEN – Page 53
ALWAYS THE WAITRESSES – Page 124
AMAZE BALLS – Page 56, AMBASSADOR TRIPLE BILL – Page 84
AWKWARD REACH – Page 87
BABS IN PAN'S PEOPLE (Top Of Our Pops) – Page 34
BECAUSE SHE WAS THE ONE – Page 38
BEEHIVE and BOUTONNIÈRE (Crossing You In Style) – Page 110
BENCHING BARRY WHITE (Langers And Mash) – Page 83
THE BEST POSSIBLE VERSION – Page 45
BIG STRONG TOYS (For Big Strong Boys) – Page 98
BIG CHEESE COMES A CROPPER – Page 55
BINARY SCHMINARY – Page 70
BLANCMANGE DILDO INSTALATION (Farts For Farts Sake) - Page 30
THE BLESSED EDDIE – Page 91
BOBSLED SKID MARKS (One Good Run) – Page 96
BOUNCING CHEQUES ON THE GHOST OF CHRISTMAS PRESENT - Page 32
BREAKDOWN IN CUSTODIAL SERVICES (Dear Oh Dear) – Page 26
CACKLING OVER CAULDRONS – Page 90
CALLING INTERPLANITARY DAFT – Page 125
CANTEEN FOOD – Page 41
CASANOVA'S CODPIECE – Page 62
CHEESE PLATTER HOST – Page 28
CLEAN UP IN AISLE 6 (Avoiding Hell) – Page 44
CLEAN SLATE (I Bet Holly Rocks) – Page 112
COMMON DECENCY – Page 31
THE CORRECT OPINION – Page 126
CREAMY ACQUISITIONS – Page 59
CRINGE AT THE CRAVING (Actually Take Back Control) – Page 69
DESK CLERK DRESSED IN BLACK – Page 88
DIDDLEY DADDY (Brenda's Concern) – Page 42

SHARP INHALE - INDEX
(Poem Titles in Alphabetical Order, Continued)

ELIZABETH BENNETT SEXES UP THE DRAPES (Obi-Wan Too Many)
- Page 29
EMANCIPATED TRUPENNY BITS – Page 118
EMILY BLUNT'S BATH WATER (Embracing Allure) – Page 63
EMPEROR PALPATINE'S SKIN-MOISTURIZING TECHNIQUES – Page 80
A FAILED PYROMANIAC CURSES ANTS – Page 93
FINDING ROOM FOR A SUNDAE MAE WEST – Page 24
FLOOR PLAN FOR SOPHIA LOREN – Page 12
FUCK FEAR, LOOK AFTER YOUR TEETH and BUY PROPERTY – Page 18
GARRY GUBBINS BUYS AN INTERBALLISTIC MISSILE ON E-BAY – Page 15
GENESIS GETS A RHYTHM SECTION – Page 122
GIFT IDEAS FOR HENRY VIII'S SIX WIVES (The Wonder of Men Part 7)
- Page 22
GLAD RIDINGS – Page 20
GLASSHOUSE EXCUSES (Seeking Out A Dream) – Page 68
GOD'S MAN CAVE (So Very Far Away) – Page 17
THE GREAT RESET – Page 128
HAND TOWELS FOR PONTIUS PILATE (An Unholy Mess) – Page 89
HILL OF BEANS - Page 74, HIP TO BE SQUARE – Page 13
HUMBUG TAMED – Page 47
ICE STATION CANCER and LIBRA (Keep Calm and Covid On)
- Page 57
ILLUMINATED USHERETTES – Page 15
IN CASE OF EMERGENCY (Mothering Deal) – Page 27
INITIALLED POCKET MIRROR (Good News For All Men) – Page 92
THE INTELLECTUAL BOLLOX OF FINNEGANS WAKE – Page 26
IT'S ENTIRELY YOUR FAULT
(A Love Poem From A Husband To His Misaligned Wife) – Page 71
I'VE NEVER SLEPT WITH HARVEY WEINSTEIN, THOUGH GOD KNOWS
I'VE TRIED (In The Dock With A Hollywood A-Lister) – Page 94
JACK SHIT and HIS JACKPOT – Page 50
KEEP IT RIGHT THERE Y'ALL (Average White Boys) – Page 97
KEEPING YOUR HOPES UP – Page 36
KING and QUEEN of POSSIBILITY – Page 75
LIAR SPIEL (Vacant Plot) – Page 120

SHARP INHALE - INDEX
(Poem Titles in Alphabetical Order, Continued)

LIMERICK LACKING – Page 73
LINEAR MULLET HICCUP (Space Time and Hair-Dos) – Page 16
A LITTLE OFF-COLOUR – Page 61
LORD OF THE MINGS – Page 100
LOST THE PLOT – Page 81
LOVE CANNOT WAIT (The Wonder Of Men – Part 122) – Page 131
LOVE ISLAND: Ancient Egypt – A Rough Week – Page 115
MAN OF THE HOUR (Unclogging Pipes with Big Ladders) – Page 72
MARTYRED FOREVER (Chide Abide) – Page 95
MATE'S RATES – Page 114
MEMORY STICK THAT STAYS – Page 49
MEL BROOKS and ANNE BANCROFT – Page 127
MICHAELANGELO MODE (Costume Fitting For Wonder Man) – Page 53
MIRRORBALLS and FRUITCAKE – Page 116
MOMMY DEAREST (Gateaux Sponges and Rock Buns) – Page 125
MUCH TRUCK – Page 58
MUSTN'T GRUMBLE – Page 119
NEVER A DULL MALADJUSTED MOMENT – Page 65
NO LONGER ON THE GAME – Page 12
NOT ADVISABLE - Page 35
NOT BODGING THE BIG STUFF (Swimming Towards The Save) – Page 130
PARADISE PRONOUNED (Cancel Culture) – Page 108
PLANTATION SHUTTERS And TORN BETTING SLIPS – Page 48
PLAYING PATIENCE WITH THE BEATLES – Page 85
RESONATOR – Page 66
RHINO FINESSE (The Making of You) – Page 76
RICH AND ROYAL HUE (Tapestry) – Page 124
ROMEO REMOVAL PILL (Where's Elon When You Need Him) – Page 105
ROOM FOR THE FORSAKEN – Page 109
ROOSTER OUTSIDE THE HEN HOUSE – Page 78
A RUN ON FARLEY'S RUSKS (Soother Suckers) – Page 54
SAUCEPANS And DOUBLE-DIGGING – Page 21

SHARP INHALE - INDEX
(Poem Titles in Alphabetical Order, Continued)

SELF-ISOLATING BY THE COAST (Breathing In Warm) – Page 51
SHARP INHALE – Page 11
SHARKSKIN WEAVE (Old Order Got To Go) – Page 111
SHIFTY TUCO and the BULLETBELT BABES – Page 103
SHIT AT EVERYTHING – Page 60
SLITHERING IN MY ROOTS (Rinsing Mr. Deflated) – Page 106
SMILING BEGUILING – Page 43
SQUEEZING OUT SPARKS WITH GRAHAM PARKER IN STOCKHOLM – Page 82
SWELLIGANT – Page 113
TERRIBLE TWOS – Page 37
THAT SLY DARKNESS (Beating Captain Neg) – Page 99
THINGS AREN'T SO BAD AFTER ALL (The Wonder of Men – Part 1) - Page 9
TOMMY TRENCHANT and the ZEN ARCHER (Real Goose Bumps) – Page 121
TORSO BY MORE SO (The Rock And I) – Page 23
THE TRUTH TAILORED TO SUIT – Page 64
VALENTINE'S DAY (When I'm 66, Never Mind 64) – Page 86
WAH WAH WAH (Golden Years) – Page 79
WE GOT YOUR BACK – Page 101
WE LAUGH AT IT NOW – Page 104
WHERE MEN ARE MEN AND SHEEP WORRY (The Pipes Are Calling) – Page 40
WORDS OF LOVE - Page 77
WORRYINGLY FULFILLED – Page 33
YOSEMITE KEROSENE – Page 102
YOU DON'T HAVE TO BE MAD TO WORK HERE – Page 107
A ZERO TRANSPARENCY FAIRYTALE – Page 67

Printed in Great Britain
by Amazon